The Best Man

Lennox Grey

Published by **Echo Vale Press**, an imprint of JMarie & Co. Publishing LLC
www.jmariepublishing.com

ISBN (Paperback): 978-1-968115-24-1
ISBN (eBook): 978-1-968115-68-5

Cover design by Tirado Designs
Printed in the United States of America
First Edition: 2025

For the "I'd like one of each" crowd…
May your fictional beds stay crowded and your fictional
feelings stay complicated.

CONTENT NOTE

Listen...

You're about to dive into explicit sex, messy emotions, family drama, queer awakenings, panic attacks, jealousy, and a whole lot of "I can't believe they just said that."
There are manipulative exes, fractured friendships, and old secrets clawing their way to the surface at the worst possible time.

There's also a splash of kink—consensual, communicative, occasionally chaotic.

If that's your vibe, welcome home.
If not... Hallmark is that way →

You've been warned.

On a more serious note...

This book touches on grief, strained parent–child relationships, internalized shame, and the painful edges of coming out. There are moments of emotional overwhelm, panic, and past sexual regret.

I write these scenes with care, honor, and lived experience. My hope is that the heavier moments bring catharsis and connection—not harm.

PLAYLIST

- ☐ **Lost in the Light – Bahamas**
- ☐ **Come Home – Anderson .Paak feat. André 3000**
- ☐ **Bad Liar – Selena Gomez**
- ☐ **Everything I Wanted – Billie Eilish**
- ☐ **The Night We Met – Lord Huron**
- ☐ **I Found – Amber Run**
- ☐ **Heavy – Linkin Park feat. Kiiara**
- ☐ **Wicked Game – James Vincent McMorrow**
- ☐ **Gravity – Sara Bareilles**
- ☐ **Take Me to Church – Hozier**
- ☐ **Love in the Dark – Adele**
- ☐ **Youth – Daughter**
- ☐ **Only Love – Ben Howard**
- ☐ **Hold Back the River – James Bay**
- ☐ **Work Song – Hozier**
- ☐ **Bloom – Troye Sivan**
- ☐ **I Lived – OneRepublic**
- ☐ **Family – Drew Holcomb & The Neighbors**
- ☐ **Turning Page – Sleeping at Last**
- ☐ **Home – Edward Sharpe & The Magnetic Zeros**

Table of Contents

PROLOGUE

Three Years Ago
Jones...

"This was the best fucking wedding week ever! *Epic, baby!*" Derrick hollers, Simone still clutched in his arms.

Derrick's my best friend, Sevynn's son—and yeah, that makes me sound ancient, but Sev's the kind of woman who doesn't age so much as sharpen. He's the one who is marrying Simone, and they're both blissfully drunk, stumbling into each other as we head to the elevators. It's the cutest damn thing.

Considering how fast they got together—months, not years—they actually work. Like magnets that found the right poles after too long repelling everything else.

I've been recording them all night, recording everyone. That's my thing. I like keeping proof that joy exists, even if it comes out grainy and off-balance. I've always been the "on" one, the guy with the camera, the jokes, the deflections. Maybe that's who I became, so no one had to see the mess behind it.

And tonight's no different. Even if my head's still spinning from what went down upstairs.

Jaxon Moore—yeah, *that* Jaxon Moore—Sev's ex-husband and some semi-famous actor, decided to hijack the wedding week with a PR stunt, dragging Sev and the kids right into it. She's had panic attacks for as long as I've known her, but this one… this one gutted me to watch. I wanted to stay, ground her, hold the damn world still for her.

But that's probably not my job anymore. Not really. Not since London. Not since everything changed.

So here we are instead. The bar. One last night of chaos before the happy couple walks the plank tomorrow.

"Jones! You're the best co–best man ever." Derrick staggers over, throws his arms around me. "Love you, man."

Derrick is a big guy. Attractive in that book boyfriend, touch her and die, kind of way. I'm tall, and he still towers over my six-foot-two frame. He smells like whiskey and lemons, which is a very odd combination, but who am I to judge?

"Love you too, baby boy. Go get some damn sleep, or you're gonna be late to your own wedding."

"I won't be sleeping tonight, *that's* for sure." He winks before pulling Simone in for a deep, very public, *way-too-much-tongue* kiss.

Heterosexuals and their PDA. I swear.

Then they're stumbling off toward their Uber. I keep filming, grinning like an idiot, watching them weave into the blur of city traffic until the taillights disappear.

I'm just about to stop recording when…

"I want to stay in your room, Jonesie. Everyone's going to a room with somebody, and no one's in *my* room."

Marley.

My heart stops. Then kicks back in twice as hard.

He's standing there in that half-drunk, half-innocent way of his—Sevynn's youngest, all soft edges and unsure smiles. Too young, too complicated, too *off-limits*.

"Fine," I say, because my mouth betrays me faster than my brain can stop it, "but I don't have sex with drunk straight men, Marley baby."

Christ, that's a rule. One that I'm aching to break.

Because the truth? Marley's not as straight as he pretends to be. He's straight for public consumption—like so many men raised in the kind of world that loves them conditionally. He doesn't say it out loud, but I see it.

And me? I clawed my way out of that closet. I'm not going back in for anyone. Doesn't stop me from shameless flirting—or the occasional late-night fantasy.

Before I can pocket my phone, Marley snatches it, shouting into the camera, way too close. "Did you all hear that? He calls me *Marley baby!*"

"Unhand my phone, young man," I say, mock outrage coating every syllable.

He grins, sheepish and glowing, that sweet-boy smile that's gotten too damn dangerous lately. I feel it low in my gut.

"I'll get us a ride home," I tell him, snatching the phone back. I point toward the benches near the exit. "You—sit. Be a good boy."

His eyes immediately went wide. "Fucking hell, Jones." He runs a hand through his hair, muttering but obeying, and sits.

Keep it PG, Jones. What the hell are you doing?

Marley's not just anyone. He's Sevynn's kid—my best friend's son. The boy I watched grow into a man I have no business wanting.

I keep my distance until the Uber pulls up, and we slide in side by side. He's quiet now, and I can't tell if it's the booze or my mouth that ruined the mood.

"You good, Marley baby?"

"Huh?" His eyes flick between mine and the back of the driver's head. "Yeah. I'm good."

He turns toward the window, watching the city lights blur into gold streaks. His reflection in the glass looks older than he is — tired and uncertain, but so fucking beautiful.

By the time we make it back to the hotel, the silence between us is thick enough to choke on. His steps falter down the hallway, almost measured, like he's walking the plank.

We're on the same floor, just a couple of doors apart. Too close for comfort.

I pull out my phone and hit record — my defense mechanism, my proof, my alibi. *Evidence for blackmail,* I joke to myself, though my pulse doesn't get the memo.

When I open the door, Marley follows like he's done a hundred times. Shoes off. Socks next. Then come the pants.

Jesus Christ.

Sevynn is going to kill me if she finds her son half-naked in my room.

"Marley baby, put your clothes back on. This isn't the—uh…"

Fucking hell. His dick is hard. Why is his dick hard?!

I drag a hand over my mouth, pretending it's not to wipe sweat or drool — anything to avoid staring. Then I make the mistake of looking up. His eyes are locked on mine, dark and hungry.

"You realize you're standing in my room with a hard cock right now, Marley baby?"

"Yes."

Just that. *Yes.* A word that unravels the last of my common sense.

Doing my best to de-escalate this sudden escalation, I manage, "Do you want to just get some sleep on the couch? I'll get you some sheets."

"Couch sheets are lava. I'm coming to bed with you."

The fuck you are!

"I'm not having sex with you."

I can't. I can't. *Fuck,* I can't.

He looks at me like that word means nothing, like rules are made for other people. "Don't you not find me attractive, Jones? I find you so fucking attractive, it makes my head spin."

Nope. Absolutely not. Abort mission.

"Let's get some sleep, baby boy." My voice cracks at the edge of calm. I led him toward the bedroom, every nerve on high alert. Sweat is everywhere—neck, palms, soul. Jones does not do sweat, baby. But there I was—*perspiring*. Gross.

"Don't call me Derrick's pet names," he says, voice low but clear. "I'm *Marley baby* to you. Always… Marley baby."

I'm rendered speechless. What do you even say to that? I swallow. Nod. Pretend that word doesn't hit me like a promise I'm not allowed to keep.

I forget I'm even holding my phone until Marley snatches it again, grinning like a drunk little devil. He sing-songs into the camera, "I'm going to sleep in Jones' bed naked, with a hard dick. I wonder if I can get him to suck it… or if he'll let me suck his."

My head whips around so fast I almost dislocate something. I snatch the phone out of his hand and kill the video.

"Marley, you can't say shit like that."

"Why?"

"One—you're drunk. Two—you're *straight*." I toss in the air quotes. "Three—you're Sev's *too-young* son."

He tilts his head. "I'm twenty-three. You're thirty-three."

He starts toward me in slow, agonizing steps, fisting himself like it's punctuation. And for the first time in our ridiculous flirt-fest, *I'm* the one cornered.

I've always been the teaser—the safe flirt, the comic relief, the man who knows when to stop. But right now? He's got me in a chokehold that I can't joke my way out of. That confidence in him—hungry, reckless—has me so hard I can barely think.

Before my brain catches up, he's pressed me back against the wall. Close enough that I can taste the whiskey on his breath.

"You've been teasing the fuck out of me for years," he says, eyes locked on mine. "So, here I am, *Jones baby*. What are you gonna do about it?"

Before I can answer, he grabs my hand, wrapping it around his cock, then guides it over mine. He sets the pace, forcing me into his rhythm while never breaking eye contact.

Who the fuck is this Marley? Where's the bashful, blushing man I've been tormenting with flirtation and safety nets for years?

I glance down at our hands, slick and moving in sync. His abs tighten. His hips roll in small, restrained thrusts that make my breath stutter.

Then his other hand slides up, firm, closing around my throat.

"Eyes on me, Jones." The command is so fucking sexy and impossible to disobey. His grip tightens just enough to hold me there, not to hurt, but to claim the moment.

For a split second, I think about pulling away—about all the reasons this shouldn't happen. Sevynn. His age. The years between who we were and this.

But before I can move, before I can form another excuse, his mouth is on mine.

And everything I swore I wouldn't do—I'm already doing.

Deliberate. Hungry. A low growl rumbles from his chest and into my mouth, and it steals every ounce of breath I have left.

I can't move. I'm too stunned, too goddamn undone by the fact that *Marley Moore*—the man I've been teasing for years— is kissing me like I'm the only thing he's ever wanted.

And then he deepens it, tongue sliding against mine, grinding closer until I can feel every frantic beat of his heart pressed into me.

By the time he pulls back, we're both panting. His pupils blown wide, lips swollen, jaw tight with determination.

He peels off my shirt like it's been offending him all night. Then his hands skim down, fumbling at my belt, his mouth dragging hot kisses along my jaw.

I should stop him. I *should*. But all I can do is lean into the fire, drowning in the sound of his growl and the taste of him on my lips.

He slowly drags his tongue under my bottom lip before pulling back just far enough to rasp, "I need to see that gorgeous fucking mouth wrapped around my cock. On your knees. Now."

Holy *shit*.

Dominant Marley is lethal and fucking dangerous. And so goddamn hot my knees nearly buckle before I even move.

There's no stopping me now. Blame the alcohol, blame the years of flirting, blame the way his eyes burn into me like I was made for this, but I'm sinking before I can talk myself out of it.

I run my tongue up his length, tracing every vein, every pulse. His cock twitches in my hand, hot and heavy, and the second I slide him past my lips, I swear my own vision whites out.

"Jones…" His voice cracks, shuddering out of him. "Oh… *ffffuuuck*."

He bows forward, one hand braced against the wall behind me, the other fisting my hair hard enough to sting. His hips jerk once, sharp, like he can't help himself.

"I knew it," he growls, staring down at me. "I knew that fucking mouth would be heaven. Take every inch, Jones baby."

I moan around him, the sound vibrating down his length, and he shivers—raw, guttural—like he's coming apart just from the sight of me on my knees.

And all I can think is, holy *fuck*. This is Marley. Sev's son. The one man I swore I'd never touch.

And I want every inch of him, anyway.

Marley is feral. His hips are snapping, driving deeper with every groan, his fist locked in my hair like he's never letting go. And me? I can't stop. My free hand is wrapped tight around my own cock, stroking hard and fast, the friction setting me on fire while my mouth works every inch of him.

I'm moaning around him, the sound muffled but vibrating down through him, and it makes him snarl—a rugged, wrecked sound that sends heat lancing straight through me.

"Fuck, Jones—yes, baby, just like that—don't stop." His voice is gravelly, and then he's thrusting harder, faster, fucking into my mouth like he's starving.

My eyes are watering, spit slicking down my chin, but I don't care. The more unhinged he gets, the closer I am, my own strokes matching the pace he's setting against my lips.

"Holy shit—Jones—fuck, I'm gonna—"

His warning rips through me, and that's it. I'm gone. My orgasm tears out of me with a moan that vibrates against his cock, and the sensation pushes him right over the line. He slams his palm against the wall, bucking hard, spilling down my throat as I shudder and spill into my fist.

We come together—messy, gasping, and ruined.

And when I finally look up at him, he's staring down at me like he can't believe what just happened.

Fuck, neither can I.

I've never felt shy, never felt uneasy after sex. I pride myself on being *that guy*—the one who knows he just rocked someone's entire fucking world. But now? I'm kneeling here with my hand still over my cock, looking up like I just got caught stealing candy.

Marley's eyes are locked on me, laser focused. He closes the distance and presses a soft, unexpected kiss to my lips.

"Let's sleep," he murmurs. "Cause I'm fucking you first thing in the morning."

He laces his fingers through mine and pulls me up and toward the bed. We climb in, cover up, and… lie there. Facing each other in the dark, neither of us saying a word, until sleep finally drags us under.

"JONES!"

I think I'm dead.

"JONES!"

Who the fuck is yelling?

I try to move—and regret it instantly. Pain detonates

behind my eyes.

"Ah… fuck." My hands fly to my temples. "Why are you yelling, dammit?" My tongue feels like sandpaper. My mouth is a desert.

"What the fuck did you do?"

I giggle, turning my head toward the sound. Marley's standing at the edge of the bed, sheet clutched to his chest like a scandalized debutante.

"Sweetie," I rasp, barely opening one eye, "judging by the way you're clutching that sheet over a very sexy, very naked body, I'd say the better question is—what did *we* do?"

His face drains of color. "No. No, no, no. That's not—this isn't—"

The realization hits me like a fucking Mack truck: he doesn't remember last night. He looks horrified. Eyes wide, knuckles white around the sheet like it's a lifeline.

I let out a slow breath, reaching for the glass of water on the nightstand. Mostly to stall. To buy myself a minute to swallow the ache clawing up my throat.

Because the truth is—I remember every fucking second.

"Relax," I say, slipping my emotional mask back into place. "You're adorable when you panic, but it's too early for melodrama." I even smile, though it's flimsy at best. "That's my job."

"Jones! Did we—did you—DID WE—"

"Marley baby," I cut in, voice dry as bone. "If I had your ass last night, you wouldn't be walking right now."

"Then why the fuck am I naked?"

Because you fucked my mouth like a savage returning from war.

"You stripped. Something about 'sheets are lava,' then you passed out face-first on my thigh. Romantic, really."

I grab my phone, thumb swiping to the video, and toss it onto the bed. Hoping—*praying*—something in him will spark.

I watch him. Every flicker of his eyes. Every glance at me. And when it gets to the part where he's slurring about wanting me to suck him off, he shuts the phone off like it burned him and tosses it back onto the sheets.

"Ohhhkay. So. I was very, very drunk. I am so sorry. I'll get dressed and leave now. So, so sorry."

Nothing. Just… nothing. Pretend it never happened. Back to normal, I guess.

"Don't look so scandalized, Marley baby," I say, summoning up my best grin. "You'll get used to waking up next to me, eventually."

"I'm never drinking again."

"Sure, you are. But for now—you've got a champagne toast to give, Best Man. Better go get yourself dressed before I steal the spotlight."

How the hell am I supposed to do *this*…

1 | JONES

Present Day

The kitchen was chaos. Which meant it was perfect.

I ducked around a line cook carrying a tray of raw steaks and snapped my towel at another who was dragging ass on plating. "Move it, Romeo. The risotto's not gonna fluff itself."

"Yes, Chef!" he barked, startled, and picked up the pace.

That's the thing about running a kitchen, you don't just cook. You conduct. Every ticket, every plate, every sauce ladle has to hit the note exactly when I want it. One offbeat and the whole symphony sounds like shit.

I slid up to the pass, checking garnishes. "No. No, no, no. Who put parsley on this? Did I ask for parsley? I hate parsley. Parsley's like giving someone wet grass and calling it salad. Fix it."

The cook blanched, grabbed the plate, and scurried back.

I sighed, rubbing the back of my neck. Lunch rush. Private

dining room packed with socialites sipping twelve-dollar cocktails and ordering "something gluten-free, but not too healthy." And, of course, Sevynn—out there in a sleek black dress, looking like decadence wrapped in silk.

Not that I'd noticed. Not that I'd been hyper aware since the second her name popped up on the reservation list.

It's her damn restaurant, and she still insists on booking tables like a regular customer, as if she can't just walk in and have the entire dining room flipped for her.

I've been working with Sev for twelve years now.

Twelve. Christ.

This place was her first baby, the one she actually named after herself—*Sevynn.* An elegant five-star restaurant that caters to steak-obsessed socialites and wine lists so overpriced they should come with a warning label. Burgundy tones, candlelit tables, chandeliers worth more than most people make in a month—it's the kind of place where people take pictures of the bathroom and post them online.

And tonight, marks three years since Sev and London got together. They're tying the knot next weekend, with her kids flying in tomorrow—Derrick, the oldest, and Marley, the youngest. Fittingly, it's also Derrick and Simone's wedding anniversary today, but they're still in Turks and Caicos. They'll be here in the morning, ready to dive headfirst into wedding week chaos.

I thought once Sev and London were official, once marriage was on the table, things between us would change. That she wouldn't need me the way I need her. But nothing's shifted. Not really. Except I've been carrying this huge fucking secret for three years—the night with her son—and no matter how good I am at wearing masks, I know she feels there is something I'm keeping from her.

"Order up!" Leslie yelled.

I stepped forward, checked the plate, and gave a curt nod. Perfect.

"Finally," I muttered. "Something I don't want to throw in the trash."

The server grabbed it, and I clapped my hands together, flashing a grin at the kitchen crew. "Alright, children. Let's pretend we like each other and get these last tickets out before somebody starts crying. And spoiler alert—it won't be me."

A ripple of nervous laughter broke through the clatter of pans. That's the thing about my crew—they know I'll cut them down with a smile and build them back up in the same breath. Keeps them sharp. Keeps me sane.

"Fire table twelve!" I barked, pointing at the line. "I want that halibut crisp, not cremated, and if I see one more garnish that looks like roadkill, I'll start mailing parsley to your mothers."

"Yes, Chef!" came the chorus, voices tight but quick.

The fry cook dropped a basket too hard, oil spitting up like it had a vendetta. "Jesus, Frankie, it's hot oil, not confetti!" I snapped, yanking a towel off the counter to mop the splash. "If you burn your hand, don't expect me to kiss it better."

I moved down the line, fingers skimming over plates, adjusting a sauce here, shifting a cut of meat there. Every dish a small performance, and me the director making sure nobody missed their mark.

The kitchen pulsed with rhythm—orders shouted, knives

clattering, the low hum of voices rising over the sizzle of pans. It was chaos. Beautiful, relentless chaos.

And me? I thrived in it.

"Table nine is asking for you, Chef."

I glanced up from the pass, one brow arched. The waiter looked nervous, like he was delivering bad news. "Table nine?"

"Yes, sir. Uh…Ms. Washington."

Of course. Sev. She went back to her maiden name shortly after she and London started dating.

I sighed, wiped my hands on a towel, and gave the line one last look. "You heard him, team—last tickets in five. Don't make me come back to a crime scene."

"Yes, Chef!"

I tugged off my apron, slung it over the pass, and pushed through the swinging doors. The hum of the dining room washed over me instantly—quieter than the kitchen but no less alive. Glasses clinking, low laughter, the kind of murmurs that cost a fortune.

And then there she was.

Sevynn.

Table nine. Candlelight catches the black silk of her dress, turning her skin into warm gold. Hair perfect, smile sharp enough to cut. God help me, she made *her own restaurant* look like it was built just to frame her.

She spotted me immediately, lifted her glass of wine in a mock toast. "Took you long enough."

"Some of us work for a living," I shot back, slipping into the smooth grin I always saved for her. "Others just swan in and terrorize the staff."

"Please. They love me."

"They fear you." I leaned a hand on the back of the empty chair across from her, lowering my voice. "And frankly, so do I."

Her lips quirked. "Good. Keeps you sharp."

I chuckled, even as my chest tightened. Twelve years of this dance, and she still had me wrapped around her little finger.

She stood, and I folded her into a deep hug. When she pulled back, her hand lingered on my jaw, followed by a soft kiss on my lips—just long enough to make my heart stumble.

"Missed you, Bestie."

"Missed you, Bestie," I echoed.

"Hey, Jones."

London stepped in, wrapping me up next, his hand cupping my jaw like he might actually kiss me, too. "Missed you, Bestie."

I smirked. "Careful, London baby. Once you go Jones, you don't go home."

He barked a laugh, letting me go with a pat to the shoulder. "Missed you, man. How've things been while we were gone?" He dropped back into his chair. Sev sat too, but not before tugging me down by the hand she refused to let go of—resting it in her lap like it belonged there.

They'd been gone six months, traveling. I'd been holding down the fort here—running her empire, flying to California and New York once a month to check in with the chefs and hash out menu changes. They wanted to see the world before the wedding, because Sev's opening a new spot here in Raleigh afterwards. That'll be a time-sucking beast of a project, and she knows it.

So yeah. It had been a few months since I'd seen them. Months of pretending the distance didn't gut me, only talking once a week—if I was lucky—when she broke down and called.

"Things have been smooth," I said lightly. "Only that one fire, but the fire department had it out before it spread too far."

"*Fire?*" Sev shot up straighter, eyes wide.

"Darling, relax." I waved her down with a flick of my wrist. "It was only the fire in my loins for that head chef of mine. Good God, that man is fine."

She groaned, dragging a hand over her face. "Why are you like this?"

"Genetics. Tragedy. And a flair for the dramatic." I grinned, unapologetic. "Pick whichever one makes you feel better."

She leans her head on my shoulder. "I hate you, but I missed you so much."

"A better man would be jealous of you two," London drawled, watching us with a smile that didn't quite hide the spark in his eyes.

"You absolutely should be," Sev said, sitting up and taking a sip of her wine. "I mean, have you seen this man's cock?"

"*Sev!*" I screeched, clutching my imaginary pearls. "It's not often I get out-Jonesed, holy *shit*, woman."

I glanced over at London—mouth wide open, staring at Sev like she'd just turned herself into dessert.

"How much has she had to drink?" I demanded.

"Too much," London laughed, sipping his own glass.

"Wedding stuff. Let's change the subject. Please." I shook my head, trying to scrub the grin off my face. Love-struck idiot.

"I'll pick the guys up in the morning and bring them to your place?" I asked.

Sev nodded solemnly. "Yes, Best Man. That is number one on your BMTDL."

I blinked. "My what now?"

"Best Man To-Do List." She chuckled, leaning her head back on my shoulder again. "I missed your shoulder so much."

"Get this woman home before she touches my no-no square in front of my customers," I said, pushing up from my chair with a dramatic flourish.

With another hug and another lingering kiss on the lips, they vanished out the door, and I returned to the kitchen.

I guess I should explain.

London is Simone's dad. Yes—*that* Simone. Derrick's wife.

Long story short, they hooked up the week of Derrick's wedding. Before they knew who the other was, and by the time the truth came out, it was too late—he was family. London never really went home after that, except to grab a few things he started leaving at Sevynn's place until, eventually, he just...stayed.

And surprisingly? He's been *shockingly chill* about my

friendship with Sev. Which is wild, considering he nearly carved me into bite-sized Jones bits the first time we met. Sev was mid-panic, and I'd gone to check on her at Simone and Derrick's welcome dinner a couple of years back. When the bathroom door opened, there he was—clearly fresh from having had sex. I did what I do best: went into "make him jealous" mode. All over Sev, grabbing her ass, calling her baby.

When I tell you I risked my life in that moment, I mean *Christ*, the man looked at me like he was deciding where to bury the body.

Since then, though, we've both made it clear: Sev and I are besties, nothing more. Like just now, me kissing his soon-to-be wife in front of him. Her talking about my impressive cock. (And yes, it *is*.)

Still, part of me thinks he wouldn't exactly mind watching her with someone else. Maybe I'm projecting, but he gets this look sometimes. Like a little imp perched on his shoulder, whispering in his ear. That primal flash in his eyes—like just now when Sev casually mentioned my cock.

I was, unfortunately, the audience to their hunger one night when I stayed over.

The sounds that woman made—hell, the sounds *he* made.

They apologized the next morning. I apologized right back for jacking off in the guest bedroom because of it.

Honesty really is my brand.

The truth is, there's an ease between us now. London slipped right into the rhythm of our lives like he'd always been there. Maybe it's the way he looks at Sev, like she's the first calm he's ever known. Maybe it's the quiet understanding that he'd kill for her, same as I would.

One night, after a steak night with friends, Sev had already gone off to bed. As the last guests filed out, London called over, "Have a beer with me, Jones."

We sat in the gazebo—him with that brooding, thoughtful air, and me wearing my best mask.

"I need to ask you something," he said, voice low. "And I expect full honesty."

"Always, London baby. What's on that sexy mind of yours?"

He didn't smile. "Are you in love with Sev?"

I didn't even think about lying. "Yes, sir. I am."

He held my gaze a long moment—long enough that I wondered if I'd have to fight my way out of that gazebo.

"Is there anything I need to be worried about?"

I shook my head. "No, sir. There is not."

"Explain." He leans forward; eyes locked on mine.

Fuck...

"Look, London." I take a breath, buy a heartbeat with my beer. "I'm not the man for Sev. You are. That's first and foremost."

I lean back, trying to look casual even though my pulse is hammering like a jackhammer in my chest. "I'm bisexual, as you're aware. There's never been a time in my life when I could promise forever to just one person—one gender. I'm not built that way, never have been. Sev needs someone who can give her their whole damn soul. And while she's got, like, eighty to ninety percent of mine? She deserves a hell of a lot more than I could ever give her. She knows it. I know it. I'd never risk losing her by crossing that line."

London studies me, quietly. That unnerving kind of silence that makes every word you said feel like a confession you weren't ready to make.

Then he leans forward, elbows on his knees, eyes cutting straight through me. "But you did cross it," he says, voice low. "At least once. She told me about that night."

Well, shit.

My gut drops.

"It's not how it sounds."

The truth spills out before I can stop it. "The day Sev signed her divorce papers, she came to my place in the middle of the night. We've always had keys to each other's homes, it was a habit at that point. She climbed into my bed. Naked. And I'm only human, London. Things did get… sexual. Extremely sexual. But I realized too damn late that she was drunk, and I put a stop to it. Immediately."

He doesn't blink. Doesn't even breathe. Just studies me like he's trying to decide if I'm telling the truth or digging my own grave.

"She was drunk," I repeat, quieter now.

"*You* weren't."

And just like that, all the air leaves the gazebo.

"No, I wasn't." I sigh, throat tight. Goddammit, this is uncomfortable.

"Sev is the only woman I've been sexually attracted to since my early twenties. Yes…given the opportunity with single Sev, I would've gone further that night if she hadn't been drunk. But she was. And neither of us would ever cross that line when she's with someone. Especially someone she loves as much as she loves you."

I take a deep breath and lean forward, matching his energy. "If you want us to stop being so touchy—the kissing, the lap-sitting, all of it—tell her. She needs to hear it from you. She'll respect it."

"I didn't say I was uncomfortable with it." His eyes narrow, calm but sharp. "I just wanted to know your intentions with said touchy-feely shit. She loves you, and she's affectionate with you. I'm fine with it—as long as I know who you are. And now I do."

I nod, take another drink. And because I am who I am… "Well, if you're asking me to join in, London baby… you have my number."

He groans, dragging a hand down his face. "And there it is. Fucking hell."

Since that night, he's never questioned me again. Not once.

She's sat on my lap in front of him like it was the most natural thing in the world. She kissed me—*hard*—after a particularly adult round of *Never Have I Ever*, her lips lingering just long enough to make the whole room squirm.

And London didn't say anything. He just watched, eyes tense, as if measuring me, weighing what he saw against the man I promised him I was.

One night, I had a date over. Mason—he was a sweet guy that I met at a book festival. Nerdy in the best way. Glasses that slid down his nose whenever he laughed. Sleeper build.

Sev was on fire that evening—more flirty than usual. She draped herself across me, whispered jokes in my ear, stole my drink, and licked the salt off the rim, eyes locked on mine.

London noticed. We all did.

Later, when I ducked into the kitchen for more wine, he followed. Leaned against the counter, arms folded, mouth curved in that unreadable half-smile.

"She's jealous, you know," he said, nodding toward the living room where Sev was laughing too loud. "That's why she's been extra flirty tonight. She's jealous of Mason."

I laughed it off—because that's what I do. But inside? Inside, I wondered if he was right. If the games we played, the affection, the touches—all of it—had been skating the edge of something we couldn't take back.

And then she proved him right.

Because when she said, *never have I ever straddled Jones and tongue-fucked him in front of his date,* and instead of drinking, climbed onto my lap and straddled me—in front of London and Mason—there was no denying it anymore.

She didn't hesitate. Didn't laugh it off. She kissed me, deep and filthy, grinding her hips against me like we were about to start an orgy right there in her living room.

And I... I kissed back. Moaned into her mouth. Gripped her hips, let her feel exactly how hard she made me. Let the whole damn room see it.

When she finally pulled away, Mason looked horrified.

And London? London was... *hard.* Not angry. Not

possessive. Just…turned on. His eyes locked on mine like a sniper with a target, and when he shifted in his seat to adjust himself, I saw it. I saw everything. Not an ounce of jealousy in him. Just hunger.

That was the last night I saw Mason.

He waited until everyone was gone, until the laughter died and the silence got too loud, and then he told me my bisexual lifestyle wasn't something he could handle. Not in a relationship. Not with me.

And I didn't blame him.

Sev had been out of line—crossed boundaries we never discussed—but the truth? I let her. Hell, I wanted it. I didn't stop her. I didn't even try.

I liked Mason. Really liked him. He was smart, kind, patient. He made room for me in his life without ever trying to shrink me down. But still, when Sev climbed into my lap in front of him and made a fucking spectacle out of the tension we never acknowledged, I didn't stop her. I kissed her back like we were alone. Like Mason wasn't even in the room.

So, I stopped bringing dates around after that. There didn't seem to be a point. And we never spoke of that night again. Not me. Not Sev. Not London.

But it haunted me.

Not because I lost Mason—but because I finally saw the truth of what we were, what we *are*. And I wasn't ready to admit it.

But always, at the back of my mind… was that night. Sev's weight on my lap. London's eyes on mine. Mason's heartbreak. And Marley—fuck, Marley.

I've wanted to tell her. God, so many times.

But how do you start that conversation?

Hey, by the way, I sucked your son's cock. You know, the one you told me to stop flirting with? The one you said was too young for me? Yeah. Him. Sorry, not sorry?

Yeah… no. Not exactly dinner conversation.

So, I haven't mentioned it. Any of the secrets I've been sitting on. Not once.

And nights like that one—her straddling me in front of everyone—just made it harder and harder. Because if she knew? If the truth ever came out?

I'd lose her. And I don't know who I'd be without her.

2| MARLEY

"Holy shit, Mars!"

I hear my name shouted across the terminal, and then Derrick's barreling toward me with Simone in tow—waving like we're in a damn movie montage.

Fuck. Three years.

"You look like a different fucking person, dude!" He drags me into a rib-cracking hug, slaps my shoulder hard enough to sting, then leans back and gives me a full once-over like I'm a prize steer at auction.

"What have you gained, like fifty pounds? And all of it pure muscle?" He pokes at my chest, eyes wide. "A beard? Since when do you have a damn beard? Fuck, I was supposed to be the hot one!"

Simone laughs, rolling her eyes. "He's been rehearsing a speech since we boarded. Now look at him—completely derailed."

Derrick ignores her, still circling me like he's inspecting a new model release. "Seriously, though. What happened to my scrawny little brother? Did you get lost in the wilderness and wrestle a bear or something? Did you *eat* the bear?"

"Ignore him." Simone shoves him aside and pulls me into a hug that smells like airport coffee and expensive perfume. "You're looking really good, Marley."

"Hey! *HEY!*" Derrick barks, grabbing her by the shoulders. "Don't touch him. You know what? Don't even *look* at him."

I laugh, shaking my head. Same old Derrick.

He snatches his luggage handle in one hand and Simone's in the other as we head toward the exit. "Marley Moore is *hot*. When the fuck did that happen?" he mutters, tugging her along. "Stop *looking* at him, Simmy!"

Simone just giggles, stumbling to keep up while he grumbles under his breath.

I shake my head, can't stop the grin stretching across my face.

Yeah. That felt good—better than I'd admit.

I'd been working on my body for nearly three years now. Not that I'd been out of shape before, but I needed somewhere to put all that restless energy. Somewhere to burn off the chaos in my head. And the gym became a church.

It's been three years since I've seen Jones. Nearly two years since I've seen Mom—God, even saying that makes me wince. I hate admitting it, but I hadn't been home in ages. The last time I saw her, she came to see me in New Orleans. She spent the weekend. Met the girl I told her I was dating at the time. Smiled, hugged me, flew back home, and that was that. Easy. Too easy. And I let her believe it, because it was safer than the truth.

I hadn't seen Derrick since his wedding week in Chicago. Law school swallowed him whole, Simone's residency kept her running on fumes, but we kept in touch over the phone. Crazy how fast years pass by.

I'd finally settled on a major.

By major, I mean I've been working as an executive chef at one of the most notorious restaurants in New Orleans for the past eighteen months. I closed on my first house eight months ago, and bought a car outright the next day.

I haven't told anyone. Not yet. I'm tired of the looks. The quiet sighs. The unspoken *here he goes again* every time I changed my mind, switched direction, chased something new, and let it slip through my fingers. This time, I've built something real. Solid. Mine. And for once, I want to hold it close a little longer before the questions start, before anyone gets the chance to doubt me.

So yeah, I've turned a lot around. No drinking. No late-night chaos. The last time I let a bottle near my mouth was three years ago—when I woke up in Jones' bed with a pounding head and no memory.

At the time, I thought nothing had happened. He didn't exactly lie—he tried to smooth it over, play it off like we were just drunk idiots. Which was fine. Safer and easier, I guess.

But when the memories trickled back, painful and undeniable, I realized the truth: I had kissed him. I had *topped* him. I had *wanted* him.

And he'd tried to pretend it was nothing—because I didn't remember, because I was panicking, because it was easier to let me believe we'd never crossed that line.

I felt like shit for weeks after that. Couldn't face him. Couldn't face anyone. He never said a word, never told a soul from what I know, but I still felt the weight of judgment pressing down on me, like somehow, they all *knew.*

The wedding happened later that day. I gave my speech, smiled for pictures, did my Best Man duties, and then caught the next flight out to Louisiana like my life depended on it.

And then the memories came in waves. Flashbacks that hit harder every time. His mouth. His voice. The way he looked at me. Each one hungrier than the last until the whole night was lodged in my head like a torture reel stuck on repeat.

One morning, I couldn't take it anymore. Walked into a gym on autopilot, signed the papers, and never looked back. The gym became my anchor. My punishment. My therapy. My escape.

And now… minutes from seeing him again for the first time since that weekend… It's doing shit to my head. Messing me up in ways I don't want to admit.

Because knowing I lost that part of my virginity to Jones — it's been rattling around in my skull for three years.

That night was the first time anyone had ever pulled me apart like that. The first time I'd been stripped down to nothing but fire and hunger and raw need. It was like he knew my body better than I did, like he'd been waiting years just to prove how undone he could make me.

And that's the part I couldn't shake at first. Not the orgasm, not the shock of it—but the way I lost control. The way I let go in a way I hadn't before.

And now I'm walking straight back into a conversation that never happened… carrying guilt that's been welded to my bones ever since.

Mom's got him running a gauntlet of Best Man duties because she and London are getting married this weekend. They thought it'd be "fun" to make it a whole production—like Derrick and Simone did. Except no one knows what the activities actually are, which is just cruel.

Derrick and I planned our arrivals—him and Simone from Turks, me from Louisiana—so Jones wouldn't have to make two trips. When we hit the pickup zone, his Ranger was already there, hatch up, waiting. Derrick had texted him that we were on our way out.

He spotted Derrick first, then Simone. Gave a quick wave as we headed over. Then his eyes flicked past them, scanning, like he was looking for someone else.

Looking for me.

And when he realized I'd been there the whole time, trailing just a step behind?

His whole demeanor shifted. His eyes went wide, and I swear I saw the words form on his lips… *holy fuck.*

His gaze swept me up and down, slow, the same way Derrick's had earlier at the airport—but this wasn't brotherly. Not even close.

We closed the distance, and he snagged Simone into his arms first.

"God, look at you, girl," he said, kissing her cheek. "It should be illegal to be this damn gorgeous."

Next was Derrick. He pulled him in, all back slaps and

grins. "Your mom is bridezilla. I blame you both for my impending torture this week."

And then it was me.

"Hey, Marley." He extended his hand, giving me the half-shake, half-hug two men do when they're supposed to be casual. Two men who *absolutely* hadn't seen each other's cocks.

"Good to see ya."

That was it. Quick. Clipped.

And then he pivoted—back to Simone, back to Derrick—lighting up, loud, animated, all that usual Jones flair like flipping a switch.

But I saw it. I *felt* it. Hell, they saw it too. Derrick's brows pinched together, confusion written all over his face. Simone's eyes cut to me, sharp and questioning, like she was clocking something she couldn't quite name.

They noticed the hole where the flirtation should've been. The missing piece of our usual banter. And that was the thing that gutted me—because I knew why. I knew he'd hate me after that night.

"Let's hit the road, bitches," Jones called out, slamming the hatch shut and herding us toward the truck like nothing was off.

Simone claimed the passenger seat, which left me and Derrick in the back. Forty minutes to Mom and London's place stretched out in front of me like a damn gauntlet. I buried my nose in my phone immediately—part nerves, part survival strategy. Small talk was not on the menu.

Marley: Thanks for this. You don't know how much I appreciate you.

> **RLM:** *Of course. Text me if you need me.*

Marley: *Then expect a text in 45 minutes, because the awkwardness has already begun.*

> **RLM:** *You got this. You got alllll this.*

Marley: *Idiot.*

I smirked at the screen, a little lighter for all of five seconds. Then the car lurched forward, and reality came crashing back in.

Up front, Simone and Jones had no problem filling the silence. I caught bits and pieces—her laughter bubbling like champagne, his voice low and smooth, carrying that effortless charm that made people lean in without realizing they were doing it.

It was too normal. Too easy. And all I could think was how not-normal things were going to feel the second his eyes found mine.

Meanwhile, Derrick wasn't about to let me stew in the backseat in peace.

"Why didn't you mention you'd been bulking up?" he asked, loud enough for Jones to definitely hear. "That's a hell of a body transition, man."

"Wasn't intentional at first," I muttered, eyes glued to my phone. "Just ended up being a thing."

Derrick leaned in, lowering his voice. "You good, man? You don't really seem like yourself. Haven't for a while now."

I forced a shrug. "I'm good. Just… distracted with shit. You know how it goes."

I knew this was coming. I *knew* it. I'm not the same kid they saw last time. Back then, I was reckless. Loud. Joyful. Stupid, even. Now? I've sanded all those edges down. Too much, maybe. And I know I'm going to have to answer this same damn question all week—*what happened to you, Marley?*

"Okay." Derrick's tone softened, and he tapped my knee. "I'm here if you want to talk, though."

"I appreciate it, Ricky. I'm good."

Simone glanced back at me, then over at Derrick. They didn't say anything, but they didn't need to. The look was enough.

And I hated it.

I sank deeper into my seat, let my phone shield me, and kept quiet for the rest of the ride.

Pulling up to Mom and London's place was like pulling up to a damn mansion. I knew they'd built a new house on the land, but *fuck*, this was way more than I expected. Big-ass driveway, three-car garage, stone everywhere like some HGTV shit.

"Shit, this place is insane," I muttered under my breath.

"Wait till you see the inside." Derrick laughed, smug. "They even have a pool house out back. And dibs, bitch."

"Motherfucker." I punched him in the chest, both of us cracking up.

We got out, and I just stood there for a second, trying to take it in. Huge porch, giant windows, perfectly cut grass. Even the damn bushes looked like they had a personal barber. Clearly, London knew what the hell he was doing—the guy designed this himself, and it shows.

Inside was even crazier. High ceilings, a big staircase, and a chandelier so over-the-top it looked like it belonged in a Vegas casino. Floors polished to a mirror shine, everything smelling like new wood and expensive candles.

The living room was all leather couches and wide open space; the kitchen had an island the size of my old dorm room. It was fancy as hell but still felt lived in—like Mom had already staked her claim with throw blankets and candles everywhere.

I let out a low whistle. "Yeah… they're doing alright."

"Honey, we're home!" Jones bellowed from the entryway.

"Oh, shit!" Mom's voice came back, followed by a loud crash and hurried footsteps. "You're early!" Another crash.

Jones smirked, already heading for the fridge. "They were definitely fucking," he stage-whispered, grabbing four beers and handing them out like party favors.

"Jesus Christ," Derrick groaned, covering Simone's ears even though she was laughing.

Jones shoved a bottle into my hand. "Beer?"

"Thanks." I handed it right back. "I'll just grab water."

Three sets of eyes landed on me like I'd just announced I was joining a monastery.

"What?" I frowned. "I don't drink anymore. Don't make it a thing."

"I'll do a water, too," Simone says, though I hate that she's giving up her beer in solidarity.

Mom and London came rushing down the stairs like they'd been caught red-handed. Mom's hair was a frizzy mess, her cheeks still flushed, and London was tugging a shirt over his head as he tried to play it cool.

Mom zeroed straight in on me and Derrick, arms flung wide. London made a beeline for Simone, pulling her into one of his big bear hugs.

"Good God, Marley!" Mom screeched, practically crushing me and Derrick in a vice of a hug. She leaned back to look me over, her eyes wide. "You're bigger than *London* now. And you have a beard!"

"Ugh. Mother." Derrick wriggled free, rolling his eyes. "So, he's the hot one now. *We get it.*"

Mom ignored him completely, her hands already up in my face, tugging at my short beard and brushing through the hair I'd let grow out past my shoulders. "Look how handsome you are, baby."

I ducked my head, grinning even as my ears burned. "Mom…"

Behind us, Jones was snickering into his beer, and Derrick muttered, "Unbelievable," like he was the forgotten child in a soap opera.

"Jones," Mom snapped, pointing at him like she'd caught him red-handed. "Did you sexually harass him all the way here? I just *know* you did."

I cut her off before things got more awkward than they already were. "I need a tour of this house, Mom. This place is crazy."

London reached for me as I pulled him into a bear hug, his laugh low and warm. "Really good to see you, Marley. And your mom's right—you're looking pretty damn good."

"Et tu brute! *London!*" Derrick threw his hands up,

spinning in a slow circle like he was performing for an imaginary camera crew. "You're all traitors. Every last one of you."

"You're still sexy to me, baby," Simone said, rubbing his face with both hands like she was kneading dough. *"Sooooo sexy. Muah, muah."*

"That's my girl," Mom said, smacking Simone's palm in a high five.

London chuckled, clapping his hands once. "Alright, tour it is. Let's go before Derrick starts a full-blown monologue."

He led the way, and I trailed behind, soaking it all in.

The living room opened up huge and airy, walls lined with windows that showed off the backyard and pool Derrick had bragged about. The kitchen was ridiculous, with double ovens and a fridge that looked like it belonged in a restaurant instead of a house.

"Jesus," I muttered. "You guys live like Kardashians now?"

"Only with less Botox and more barbecue," Jones quipped, leaning on the counter with his arms crossed over his chest.

I glanced at him. Too quick. Then looked away, pretending I hadn't heard him at all.

The dining room was all elegance—long mahogany table, chandelier overhead, candles already set like Mom had been waiting to throw a dinner party.

Upstairs, London pointed out the guest rooms that we'd all be staying in, the balcony off the master, and when we circled back down, he pushed open the doors to the back patio. I use the word patio loosely; it's practically a football field. The pool glowed under string lights, with the pool house tucked off to the side like it was its own mini-mansion.

"Dibs," Derrick reminded me, smirking as he slung an arm around Simone.

"Asshole," I muttered, shaking my head with a grin.

3| JONES

Fuck, he's acting like *I'm* the one who forgot that night. Like, *yeah*, it's awkward, but the way he's looking through me? Borderline pissed.

And pissed at what? If Marley wanted to talk about what happened with us, talk about anything he's been up to over the past three years, he could've picked up the phone sometime in the last three years. He didn't. So why should I be the one to drag it into the light? Safer to leave it buried. Cleaner. Easier.

But Christ, seeing him again—it's wrecking me. His hair is longer now, falling onto his face in a way that made me want to push it back. Broader shoulders, chest filling out that T-shirt like he's been living in the damn gym. The scruff suits him too—grown, sharp, dangerous in a way he never was before.

And black. All black. Henley pulled tight over that new body like he *knew* exactly what kind of weapon he was walking around in.

There's nothing left of the old Marley. Not even his personality. The reckless, grinning, young, immature man I used to tease is gone. And in his place is a man who's going to ruin me all over again. A man who belongs to the woman who ruins me every fucking day.

I love this for me. Truly. Gold stars.

"Jesus," he muttered, looking around. "You guys live like Kardashians now?"

"Only with less Botox and more barbecue," I shot back, slipping into the familiar rhythm, trying to lighten the air, drag us back into our usual banter. Normalcy.

He barely glanced my way. Blank. Like I hadn't said a damn word.

And just like that, I felt the heat crawl up my neck. Now *I'm* the one pissed.

London continued the tour, but I stayed behind. Let them ooh and ahh over the guest rooms and the balcony—I'd seen enough.

Through the glass doors, Sev was outside, already in hostess mode, getting the meat ready for the pit now that people were starting to trickle in. London's brothers, Marcus and Joe; and his sister, Sloane, would be here in a couple of hours. His parents rolling in tomorrow morning.

It's been nice watching her with them. Watching her finally have the big, noisy family she always craved. Simone slips right in like the daughter she always wanted, and London's brothers give her the same kind of grief they give him—teasing, protective, loud. It's good for her. It makes her shine.

But lately, I've been feeling out of place.

When it was Sev and Jaxon, I knew my role. Hell, I *was* her role. At her side, because he sure as hell wasn't. It was her and me against the world, and I was good at that. Needed, wanted, irreplaceable.

But now… she's got her own family. Her own people. A new orbit. And I'm not sure I belong in it anymore.

And the worst part? Once she finds out about what happened between me and Marley, I'll lose her, anyway. No more best friend, no more anchor, no more *us*.

So maybe it's better to start creating that distance now. Rip the Band-Aid slowly before the whole damn thing tears open.

I've been looking at different places further south. There's a restaurant in Houston I've had my eye on, and a couple weeks ago they reached out about an interview. I've built a name for myself since Sev won her last Michelin star—headhunters popping out of the woodwork like roaches in the dark.

Maybe distance is what I need. Build my own life instead of living in hers.

I'm turning thirty-five this year. No kids. No ring. No family. My parents died when I was fourteen, and they were both only children. So, no aunts, no uncles. Which meant foster care for me. And no one adopts teenage boys, not really. I aged out at eighteen with no one in my corner.

No one… until Sev.

I met her when I was twenty-three. By then, I already knew cooking was it for me. I'd done most of the meals in our group home, helping the ladies who ran it. Started sneaking in recipes I'd found online or in old library cookbooks, blowing my summer-job money on herbs and spices nobody could pronounce. I wanted elegance. Sophistication. Art on a plate—even if I was serving it off paper plates in a kitchen that smelled like bleach and boiled cabbage.

I bounced around a while—busboy, dishwasher, line cook in hole-in-the-wall spots. And then I landed at Sevynn. Her dream. Her first baby.

The night before her grand opening, her executive chef got arrested.

I can still see her—hair wild, pacing the kitchen, gripping her phone like it was a lifeline.

"I can't. I can't fucking breathe," she kept muttering. "It's too much. I don't have a head chef. I can't do this without a chef."

"Chef?" I stepped forward, back straight, hands behind me in mock military pose.

She looked at me like I'd grown a second head. "Jones, you're the *busboy*."

"I know your menu like the back of my hand," I said calmly. "I've watched. I've studied. I know every detail."

She exhaled hard, pressing her palm to her forehead. "Jones… thank you, but you're the busboy. And it's not that I don't respect you—I do—it's just… this night is everything. I can't risk it."

"Then test me," I countered. "Ask me five questions about tonight's menu. Anything you want. If I get even one wrong, I'll go back to finishing dishes and you'll never hear from me again."

She stared at me like I'd lost my damn mind. Then, finally

she crossed her arms, narrowed her eyes, and fired off:

"Alright, Jones. First question. What wine are we pairing with the duck confit?"

"Pinot Noir, 2014 vintage, earthy enough to cut the fat but not overpower the cherry glaze." I didn't blink.

Her jaw twitched. "Fine. Second. Explain the plating for the sea bass entrée."

"Center-cut fillet over a bed of saffron risotto, microgreens fanned at ten o'clock, beurre blanc drizzled at the rim, not the fish. Gold-leaf garnish on the lemon wedge."

She blinked once. Hard. "Third. What's the difference between the amuse-bouche and the appetizer course tonight?"

"Amuse-bouche is a single bite of smoked salmon mousse on crostini, meant to set the palate. The appetizer is the wild mushroom tart with truffle cream. Amuse is complimentary; the appetizer is ordered. Timing is everything."

I could see her breathing faster now, but she pressed on. "Fourth. What temperature do the soufflés need to hit before service?"

"Three hundred seventy-five, exactly twelve minutes. Any less and they collapse before leaving the oven. Any more and they're dry. Pull them when the crown just sets, serve immediately."

Her lips parted, but no words came.

I leaned in, voice low. "One more, Chef."

She swallowed, then went for the jugular. "Fifth question. The risotto. What's the ratio, and how do you know when it's done?"

I smiled. "One cup arborio to three cups stock, added half a cup at a time, stirred until it begs for mercy. You know it's ready when it sighs off the spoon—creamy, loose, but still with bite at the center."

Silence. Just her staring at me, breath caught, hand still pressed to her chest like she was trying to keep her heart from jumping out.

I straightened, wiping my palms on my apron. "Five for five. I'll go put the dishes away now."

"Jones…" Her voice cracked just a little. "Get your ass on the line."

And just like that, everything changed.

We ran that kitchen together like a well-oiled fucking machine. It was chaos all around us—pans clattering, servers yelling "behind," tickets spewing from the printer like confetti—but between us? It was instinct. It was oxygen.

She dropped something; my hand was already there to catch it. A saucepan flared; I had it cooled before she even glanced. If her voice called "fire table twelve," mine echoed the command down the line, pushing the crew to move faster, sharper.

She missed something at the pass once, exhaustion tugging at her edges. I caught it before it ever left the kitchen.

"That's the wrong sides for the duck," I barked, snapping my fingers at the server and pulling the plate back before it was halfway through the door. The crew froze for half a second. I didn't. I had a new plate fired, garnished with micro herbs, slid it onto the silver rim, and shoved it forward.

Sev didn't miss a beat. She didn't apologize, didn't falter.

Just gave me the smallest nod, eyes blazing like fire caught in crystal. That was her thank you. That was her *I see you*.

And that's how we worked—no wasted words, no dropped balls. If she stumbled, I was already there. If I slipped, she was already covering. A machine, yes. But ours.

Two hours in, we weren't Jones and Sev anymore—we were one body with two pairs of hands, two voices cutting through the storm. Her plating was precise, my timing flawless. Every dish hit the window looking like art, and we barely spoke, because we didn't have to.

By the end of the night, when the last plate left the pass and the dining room roared with applause, I looked at her across that counter, sweat dripping down both our faces, and knew: this was it.

This was my place. My purpose.

And Sevynn… she wasn't just my boss. She was my person.

So, the thought of leaving the only family I've ever truly known—yeah, it hurts like a bitch. But what's my alternative? Stick around and third wheel her marriage until I'm eighty? Pretend I'm fine while she builds this whole new life that doesn't have a Jones-shaped space in it anymore?

I'll never be able to move on as long as I'm close enough to look her in the eyes. As long as I get to see that smile every day, the one I've lived for, the one I've chased like oxygen.

It's been my addiction since the very first night we met. When service ended and the crowd applauded, she looked at me across the pass, eyes wild, face lit up with relief and triumph—and she smiled.

That smile.

And I knew then and there I wanted to spend the rest of my damn life making her smile like that.

"Hey, you."

Her voice cut through my haze, snapping me out of staring into my beer like it held the answers. I blinked, and she was right there, crossing the kitchen toward me.

She hopped up onto the counter, casual as anything, knees parting just enough to pull me in. Her arms looped around my neck, tugging me into her orbit like she'd done a thousand times before.

"You okay?" she asked softly, head tilted, eyes searching mine.

I nodded, but it wasn't convincing. Not with the way her touch was undoing me.

"What are you thinking about?"

Before I could lie, she pressed a kiss to my jaw. Soft. Familiar. And then another, grazing the corner of my mouth before finally sealing it with her lips.

Gentle. Dangerous. The kind of kiss that made it too damn easy to forget I was supposed to be letting her go.

"The kids are gonna get the wrong idea with you all over me like this," I laughed, nervous, taking a big gulp of my beer.

"They know I kiss you all the time. What are you talking about?" She tilted her head, narrowing her eyes. "What's up with you today?"

"Nothing." I shut my eyes and shook my head hard, like I could knock the thoughts loose. *Shake it off, Jones. Jesus Christ, shake it off already.*

So, I did what I always do—deflect. "I just don't want you burning my steak again. You know I like my meat still moving, dammit."

"Wow. One time." She smacked my chest with a laugh. "One time that happened, and you've been holding it over me ever since. Name one other thing I've burned!"

She shot back, and I latched onto the banter like a life raft. And while she was laughing, I slipped just far enough out of her arms to put a little air between us.

But Sev noticed. She always notices.

Her smile softened, and instead of letting me off the hook, she leaned forward, tugging me forward by my belt until I was back between her thighs.
"No. I'm not falling for it this time. Come back here."

Goddammit.

This time, she kissed me. No hesitation, no teasing—just her hand sliding into my hair, mouth slanting over mine, tongue brushing gently like she had every right to claim me.

Fuck. I can't do this right now.

I tore myself back, retreating fast until my spine hit the opposite counter. The distance was a wall I needed—barely.

She tilted her head, eyes narrowing, studying me like I was a puzzle she'd been trying to solve for years.

"I'm going to go get the rest of the stuff for the sides for tonight," I said slowly. "Do you want something back?"

"Jones…"

"I'm okay, Sev." My voice sounded flat, wrong even to my own ears. "Do you want anything?"

She slid down off the counter and crossed the kitchen, close enough that her perfume tangled in my lungs. "Pick me up."

I did—because I always do. Her arms wrapped around my neck, legs around my waist like we always do.

"Please tell me what's wrong," she whispered. "Am I being too much?"

"No." I exhaled hard. "Yes… and no."

I set her down just as footsteps pounded back toward the kitchen. Derrick and Simone entered first, laughing about something I couldn't hear over the pounding in my ears.

"I'll head to the store," I muttered, already moving. "Text me if you want anything."

I could see the pained look on her face as I pulled away, but I just walked out without another word.

4 | MARLEY

Marley: Save me…

RLM: This isn't Smallville.

Marley: You know…I'm starting to rethink some of my life choices.

RLM: Are you, now? Well, let me know what you decide.

I smirked down at the screen, thumb hovering over a reply I didn't send. Before I could, Mom's panicked voice cut through the kitchen.

"He's still not answering."

I looked up. She was pacing, phone clutched in her hand like sheer willpower could make Jones pick up. Two hours she'd been at it, and every missed call ratcheted her anxiety higher.

London was already outside, firing up the grill, steaks lined and waiting. The table was set, the wine was breathing, and Mom was stuck in place, waiting on the one piece that hadn't fallen yet—Jones.

It wasn't like him. Not answering her? *Never* happened. And the longer it went on, the more I could see it in her—this edge, this nervous energy she was trying to disguise as irritation.

"His phone's probably just dead, Mom." I leaned against the counter, trying to sound casual. "It's *Jones*. He'll be back."

Her mouth pinched, unconvinced.

"I'll help with the sides." I slid my phone into my pocket and moved toward the pantry before she could argue. "Your pantry's massive—he probably didn't even need to go to the store."

I swung open the doors and whistled low. Rows of oils, spices, grains—everything stacked and labeled like a damn grocery aisle. "Jesus, Mom. This is overkill."

"Jones keeps it stocked," she said automatically, watching me.

I started pulling things without thinking, instinct kicking in. "Okay, we've got ribeye's and filets out there. Potatoes are a no-brainer—garlic mash, nice and creamy. Maybe some roasted asparagus, hit it with lemon zest. Oh—and that farro," I said, tugging the bag down from the shelf. "We can do a warm salad with charred tomatoes and feta. It'll balance the fat from the meat."

My hands were moving before my brain caught up, lining ingredients on the counter, sketching the whole meal in my head without even trying. It felt weirdly natural—like slipping into someone else's shoes. *His* shoes.

Behind me, I felt it before I saw it, Mom and Derrick staring holes into the back of my head.

Shit.

I hadn't even thought before I jumped in. I just wanted to help for once. But now, there'd be questions.

"MasterChef," I blurted out too fast. "That's my shit."

Derrick snorted immediately. "Oh my *God*, you did not just MasterChef your way out of this."

I shot him a glare over my shoulder. "What? I've seen every season. Twice."

"Bullshit." He stepped closer, eyeing the lineup of ingredients like they might rat me out. "You knew exactly what to grab without even looking. That's not reality TV muscle memory, Mars. That's kitchen muscle memory."

Mom leaned against the counter, arms folded, studying me like she was trying to fit new puzzle pieces into place. Her voice was softer, though. "Why didn't you tell me you've been cooking like this?"

My throat tightened. I grabbed the knife, kept my eyes on the garlic instead of Mom's face. "I follow recipes while I watch *MasterChef*, okay? And anything else Gordon Ramsay related. Man's gotten me through plenty of overcooked ramen nights."

The joke landed, kind of. Derrick huffed out a laugh, but it had that edge of disbelief. Mom tilted her head like she was filing the answer away, unconvinced but choosing not to push—at least not now.

They didn't buy it. I could feel it. But thankfully, they let it go.

For now.

The entire time I moved through the kitchen, I could feel eyes on me. Different sets at different times, like I was some animal on display.

London came in with a tray of sausage, paused mid-step, eyebrows up like *the hell is he doing?* Then he thought better of it and kept moving.

Mom hovered. Watching, not hovering like she didn't trust me—hovering like she was cataloguing every move.

Even Joe, Sloane, Marcus… all of them poked their heads in at one point, wearing the same "what the actual fuck" expression.

Like, yeah, I get it. I'm cooking. Like an adult. Big shocker. Take a picture, frame it, put it on the goddamn mantle already.

By the time I had everything plated in the fancy porcelain Mom pulled out—garlic mash, roasted asparagus, farro salad still steaming—she finally grabbed a plastic spoon. Tasted everything, one by one.

Her eyes widened. She set the spoon down like she needed both hands to process. "What the *fucking hell*, Marley. Remind me to thank *MasterChef*, because… fuck. This is *good.*"

Something hot and heavy hit my chest. Her pride. Real, unfiltered pride. Finally.

It was more than I expected to get out of this week. Hell, more than I thought I'd get from her in years.

She set the spoon down and came straight to me, arms wrapping me up in one of those bone-crushing hugs I hadn't had since I was a kid. For a second, I just stood there, stunned, then let myself sink into it.

"You don't have to tell me, Mars," she whispered, voice

low enough that only I could hear. "But I'm proud of you. Whatever it is you're too afraid to say out loud."

My throat closed, the words caught there like wet concrete.

She pulled back, eyes glassy and gentle, giving me that soft, knowing look that always manages to find the version of me I try to hide. Her hand came up, thumb brushing the line of my jaw like she was memorizing me all over again.

"It suits you," she said, a small smile ghosting across her face.

Then she leaned in and kissed my nose — the same way she used to when I was little, when scraped knees and monsters under the bed were the worst of my problems.

For the first time in years, I felt like her kid again.
Not her disappointment.
Not her worry.
Just... *hers.*

"Let's get everything to the table," she said finally, voice catching as she wiped at a tear.

She turned, busying herself with plates from the cabinet, her movements brisk in that *don't-make-this-a-scene* way only mothers have. The smell of garlic and rosemary filled the kitchen, wrapping around the moment like a blanket.

I watched her go, chest tight.
She had no idea how much I wanted to tell her everything.

About the years away.

About Jones.

About the parts of myself I'd finally stopped pretending weren't real.

But the words sat like stones in my mouth.

Instead, I pulled out my phone, snapping a quick picture of the dinner spread before the ache could get any louder.

Marley: Just call me Chef Mars…

RLM: I've seen better. Rookie.

Marley: Fuck off. That's the same farro salad I made for the competition.

RLM: Well shit. You had to take it there. Damn you. I bet they loved it. Did you tell them yet?

Marley: Not yet. Soon. Promise.

RLM: You will when the time's right. No one can make that decision but you.

The typing bubble blinked for a second before disappearing. I stared at the screen until my reflection blurred into the glow, the words *when the time's right* echoing louder than they should.

Because the time never feels right. Not when the people you love most are the ones you're most afraid to lose.

———

Dinner went smoother than I ever expected—conversation flowing easy, laughter passing around the table like bread baskets.

Mom settled, mostly. She looked lighter somehow, the tightness in her shoulders gone for once. Every fifteen minutes or so, her phone would light up beside her plate. She'd glance down, thumb hovering like she might try Jones again, then set it aside.

But she was smiling. And that was enough for me.

The house was alive again, full of the low hum of voices and clinking glasses. London and his brothers had migrated to the pool table, arguing about rules and lining up shots between jokes. Simone and London's sister had claimed the couch, bare feet propped on the coffee table as they watched *The Circle* and giggled like teenagers.

For the first time since I left, the house felt alive again—like it remembered me. Every laugh, every clink of glass stitched me back into a rhythm I didn't realize I'd missed. Even without Dad here, London slipped into that space so seamlessly it almost felt like the house had been waiting for him too.

I slipped on my walking shoes, trying to be quiet about it, though the squeak of the soles still drew Mom's eyes. She was sitting with her wineglass cradled in one hand, the flicker of the TV catching on her cheekbones.

When our gazes met, I gave her a soft smile and nodded toward the door—an unspoken invitation.

Come walk with me.

She didn't need words. Just set the glass down, smoothed her hands over her jeans, and nodded back.

There was something comforting about that small exchange—like muscle memory. Like no matter how much time had passed, she'd always understand my language of quiet gestures.

"You seem so different, Marley," Mom said softly as we eased down the front steps and started toward the walking trail.

I'd noticed it earlier from the kitchen window—the way the path curved behind the house, tucked beneath a canopy of oaks strung with tiny golden lights. Now, at dusk, it glowed like something out of a dream. London had outdone himself.

The air smelled faintly of pine and smoke from the fire pit, that mix of earth and warmth that somehow makes you feel both grounded and exposed.

"I know," I said finally, hands tucked in my pockets. "There's…"
I trailed off, watching our shadows stretch ahead of us. How the hell do you summarize three years of silence and self-discovery into a sentence that won't break her heart?

"There's a lot to catch you guys up on," I managed, voice low. "I'm sorry I've been MIA."

She didn't answer right away. The gravel crunched beneath our shoes, steady and unhurried, like she was giving me room to find the words.

"Are you and Jones okay?" I asked finally. "It's not like him to not be here. I know it's been a while since I've been around the two of you, but something feels… *off*."

She shook her head, exhaling like the question itself hurt. "That's what I'd like to know, too. I know he's been keeping something from me."

Fuck.

I do.

I stayed quiet, not even knowing what to say.

"I just don't know what or why. But he'll always be my person." She continued.

Her person. The words sat heavy in my chest.

"London okay with another man being your person?" I asked, half joking, half needing to understand.

"Yeah," she said with a small smile. "He knows how important Jones is to me."

She went quiet for a moment, the rhythm of her steps falling in line with mine. "I'm sure to the outside world, we have a very odd relationship, the three of us. But I wouldn't have it any other way. Neither would they."

A pause. Then, softly, "Well… as far as I *know*, anyway."

My heart was pounding so loud I could barely hear the crunch of gravel anymore. My palms were slick. My throat felt raw.

It was now or never.

"Mom."

She looked at me, brows pinched in that way she does when she's bracing for bad news.

I swallowed hard. "I think I know what Jones is keeping from you."

Her steps faltered, just slightly. Her eyes met mine, sharp with worry. "Is he sick?" she asked quickly, tone climbing with panic.

"No. No, nothing like that."

The relief that washed over her only made it worse.

I ran a hand through my hair, staring up at the treeline where the lights shimmered faintly through the leaves. My head fell back, and the truth clawed its way out.

"Something… *sexual*… happened between me and Jones the night before Derrick's wedding."

The words hung there, heavy and alive, like they'd taken on a pulse of their own.

For a second, the only sound was the whisper of wind through the trees. The lights overhead flickered against the leaves, throwing gold shadows across her face, and I realized I was holding my breath.

Her lips parted, but no sound came out. Then—softly, almost too quiet to hear—

"Okay."

Just that. One word.

"Are you…" I started, not sure what I was even asking.

She cut in, her voice tight. "Do you have feelings for him? For each other?"

She was wringing her hands, twisting her wedding ring round and round, eyes darting like she was trying to anchor herself to anything but the truth in front of her. And for a split second, the look on her face—hurt, confused, something sharper—felt almost like jealousy. But that couldn't be right.

"No." The word came out rough, defensive. "It was a drunken night I barely remember, and I was ashamed. Please don't blame him."

I swallowed hard, forcing the rest out before I lost my nerve. "I was a hundred percent the aggressor, and nothing's ever happened before or since. But if it's been eating at him even half as much as it's eaten at me all these years…"

My voice cracked.

"I can imagine that's the thing he's been keeping from you."

"Let's keep walking."

Her steps quicken, the sound of gravel sharper now, like punctuation between every thought she's not ready to say.

"Mom."

Nothing.

"Mom." I reach out and catch her wrist, stepping in front of her. "Mom, talk to me."

She stops short. Her eyes are glassy, wide and unfocused, like she's looking somewhere behind me instead of at me.

For a moment, I think she's going to pull away—but instead, I pull her in. She feels small in my arms, all tension and tremor. I rest my cheek against the top of her head, the scent of her shampoo suddenly achingly familiar.

"You have feelings for him, don't you?"

Nothing. Just her breath catching against my chest.

"Does London know? Are you having second thoughts about the wedding?"

"No!" She shakes her head hard, the word breaking apart halfway through it. I feel her wiping tears with the back of her hand before she wraps her arms around me in return.

"It's complicated," she says finally, voice low, frayed at the edges. "And probably not a conversation I should be having with my son. It just… shocked me, is all."

Complicated.

The word ricochets in my head.

Complicated.

Fuck.

Are the three of them…?

Ugh. I do not want to know.

"I'll say this, and then we never have to discuss it again," I said, holding up a finger. "In fact, I'll be searching for one of those memory guns from *Men in Black.*"

That earned a soft chuckle. She reached over and pinched my side.

"Happiness looks different for different people," I went on, rubbing the spot she'd pinched. "Anyone with eyes can see how you all feel about each other. If that's what happiness looks like to you, Mom, don't let something that happened three years ago in a drunken stupor stop you from being happy. Even if it does make Thanksgiving a little awkward."

Another pinch.

"Ah—fuck! Keep your talons to yourself, woman!" I laughed, pressing a quick kiss to the top of her head. "How the tables have turned."

She laughed too, finally — that deep, easy laugh that always managed to knock the air right out of me.

"I mean…" I couldn't help myself. "What will the grandkids call him? *Poly-Pop?*"

Her mouth dropped open in mock horror.

Before she could retaliate, I bolted down the trail. "*Papa-Poly!*" I yelled over my shoulder, grinning as her footsteps pounded after me.

"Goddamnit, Marley Moore!" she shouted between laughs. "Get your ass back here!"

The sound of her laughter chased me through the trees — bright, wild, and familiar in a way that made my chest ache. By the time I hit the back door, I was breathless, doubled over and grinning like an idiot.

I barely made it inside before she strolled in behind me, cool as ever, like that hadn't been a damn near mile-long sprint.

"Help!" I yelled, stumbling into the living room.

London looked up from his game of pool, one brow arched, already wearing that knowing smile that said *you brought this on yourself.* Derrick, Marcus, and Joe turned, eyes darting between us like they'd just been handed front-row seats to a family brawl.

"She's such an angry gremlin!" I said, pointing at Mom.

Her expression didn't budge, but that wicked spark in her eyes told me I was a dead man walking.

"Get him."

That was all it took.

Derrick whooped, Marcus cracked his knuckles for dramatic effect, and Joe just grinned like this was his moment to shine. Before I could even get the word *wait* out, they were on me — three grown men dragging me toward the sliding glass door, laughing like lunatics.

"Not fair!" I yelled, thrashing like a wet cat. "You're supposed to protect me, not participate!"

"Dunk him, boys!" Mom called, her laughter ringing out as

Simone and Sloane's giggles joined in from the couch.

"Traitors!" I shouted, just before the world tilted and a rush of cold swallowed me whole.

The pool water hit like ice, stealing the air right from my lungs. I surfaced to the sound of cheers and cackling, hair plastered to my face, sputtering.

Mom stood by the pool, hands on her hips, smug as hell.

And for all the chaos, all the noise, all the goddamn soaking humiliation—I couldn't stop laughing.

By the time I'd dried off, swallowed my pride, and officially admitted defeat, the house had settled into that easy hum it always had after dinner—music low, glasses clinking, voices overlapping from every direction.

Everyone had migrated to the game room, drawn like moths to the neon glow of the air hockey table.

London bought it for their one-year anniversary—a nod to their first date, when he and Mom had gone to one of those retro arcades and nearly got kicked out for taking the competition a little *too* seriously.

This one, though, wasn't some cheap plastic setup from a sporting goods store. It was a four-player monster—solid mahogany base, chrome trim, the works. Their names were etched along the sides in clean, looping script: *Sevynn & London*. A fucking monument to love and bragging rights.

Trash talk started before anyone even touched a paddle.

Simone had already planted herself at one end, chin high, declaring, "I'm reclaiming my crown tonight. Queen of the Table is back, peasants."

Derrick groaned, swearing vengeance for last year's so-called *Christmas massacre*.
"Not this time, woman. I've been training."

Their laughter bounced off the walls, filling every corner with warmth.

I hadn't been home for the holidays in years. Watching them now, it hit me how much I'd missed this—how much they'd missed *me*. I tried not to let that ache bleed through, but it lingered under my grin all the same.

London pressed a kiss to Mom's lips as he set his cue stick down. "I need to run an errand," he murmured, then turned back toward us with a grin. "Don't let her win. It goes to her head."

"Operation Don't Let Mom Win—commence!" I declared, full of mock authority, grabbing the puck and spinning it on the table like I was about to face off in the Stanley Cup finals.

I shot her a grin. "Alright, Mighty Gremlin. Let's see what you got."

Her eyes lit up, that mischievous spark that always meant trouble. "You're about to regret every life choice you've ever made, Mars."

Derrick groaned from the couch, nursing his drink. "God, she always says that."

"Yeah," Simone added, laughing, "and somehow, she always wins."

"Not tonight." I smirked, bouncing from foot to foot as I leaned over the table, adrenaline buzzing in my chest.

She won….

Every. Goddamn. Game.

Against me. Against Simone. Against Derrick, who swore he was "going easy." Against Joe and Marcus, when they decided two-on-one would even the odds.

Didn't matter.
One by one, we went down like bowling pins.

Whoever let this woman into an arcade owes us all a formal, written apology.

The air was thick with laughter and curses, the motor of the table humming under it all like a taunt. When the final puck ricocheted off my goal with a humiliating *clang*, she snatched it mid-bounce, strutted to the center of the table, and dropped it like a mic.

"Boom," she said, grinning like a full-blown villain.

I groaned and dropped my head against the rail, voice muffled. "I fucking hate it here."

That set everyone off. Simone doubled over, Derrick wheezed, and Marcus nearly fell off his stool. The sound filled every inch of the room until it felt like the walls themselves were laughing with us.

And Mom?
She just tossed her hair back, shining in the neon light, basking in her undefeated glory like a queen surveying her conquered kingdom.

For a minute, it was easy to forget everything else—the time, the guilt, the weight still sitting in my chest.

For a minute, we were just *us*.

5 | JONES

Sevynn has called eighteen times in six hours.

Eighteen fucking times.

I don't know what the hell I was thinking—disappearing like that. I've never felt this panicked about her before. Everything between us has always been easy. Even with how much I love her, we just… fit.
And London allowed us to fit.

But now that they're getting married, I know I'm the odd one out.

She doesn't need me anymore. He's the one who can pull her out of panic attacks with a word, who can steady her shaking hands when I used to have to hold her through them. He's helping her design the new restaurant, making choices I used to help her shoulder.

And don't get me wrong—it's not jealousy. I swear to God, it's not. I want every damn good thing for her. Every joy, every victory, every goddamn smile.

It's just… I don't *fit* anymore.

And the longer I keep pretending I do, the worse it's going to hurt when that truth finally sticks.

I didn't even go to the store like I told her. I came home. Couldn't sit there and laugh and play along like everything was normal.

Because what happens if she tries to kiss me again like she did earlier?
Everyone laughs it off—that's just us, right? That's *our thing*. But fuck, it makes us look like some kind of throuple. Or worse, like I'm her bisexual sidekick hanging around for scraps of her attention.

So I paced. An hour, maybe more.
Back and forth across the living room, phone in hand, thumb hovering between calling her back or throwing the damn thing across the room.

The air was thick—humid, restless. My chest hurt from holding too many words inside.

I didn't get the chance to decide, because a knock at my door froze me in place.

When I opened it, there he was.

London.

Well. Yay fucking me.

"Let's talk…" His voice was even, but his eyes didn't flinch. He stepped back just enough, leaving it on me—was I going to invite him in, or was I going to run?

"Yeah. Sure." My voice didn't sound half as casual as I wanted it to. I moved aside, letting him pass. He walked in with that calm authority he always carried, like the whole damn world bent a little to make space for him. The door clicked shut behind us, heavy as a verdict.

London turned, arms crossed, leaning against my counter like he owned the place already. "You want to start talking," he said, voice low but steady, "or should I?"

I looked him over, and Jesus Christ—he was every bit the warning label he looked like.

Biceps flexed beneath the stretch of a black henley, cap turned backward, jeans that did dangerous things for his thighs. Casual, sure. But it wasn't comfort—it was control. He looked like he could break my neck and then fix it just to do it again.

I swallowed hard, scrubbing a hand over my face to buy a few seconds. My pulse was hammering so loud it almost drowned out the hum of the refrigerator.

"Guess that depends," I muttered finally, letting my hand drop. "Am I about to get the *protective fiancé* lecture, or the *concerned friend* one?"

The corner of his mouth twitched—almost a smirk, almost a snarl.

"I haven't decided yet," he said.

Well, *that's* fucking worse.

I dropped onto the couch opposite him, leaning forward with my elbows on my knees. My hands dangled between them, restless, my fingers rubbing against each other like they were trying to find something to hold onto.

"It's getting to be too much," I said finally, the words rough around the edges. "For me. All of this." I motioned between us, between the space that held her, too, even if she wasn't here. "I don't fit in your lives anymore, Lon." My voice cracked on his name. "And I sure as hell won't when you're married."

The words burned on the way out, but I forced them. "There isn't a damn thing I can give her that you and your family can't. She doesn't need me anymore. And I…" My throat locked up, eyes stinging. I blinked hard, swallowing it down, like maybe I could push it back where it belonged.

"I just need to start building my own life," I finished, softer. "That's all. And it's… It's hitting me harder today than usual." I dropped my gaze, shaking my head. "I'm sorry if I ruined dinner."

The silence that followed was heavy as stone, like the air itself was waiting to see whether London Pierce was going to break me in half or… something else.

"You done?"

"That's my line, you ass." I tried for humor, but it came out thin and brittle.

He just stood there, full of all his infuriating *London-ness*, pinning me in place.

"Yes, I'm done," I muttered, finally.

"There is no Sev without you," he said evenly. "And there is no you without Sev. I knew that a week after meeting the two of you. You're family, Jones. *More* than family. What is it you don't understand about that?"

I opened my mouth, but he cut me off with a raised hand.

"You say you don't fit. But you know what was at *our* dinner table tonight? A huge, gaping fucking hole. One that only *you* fill. This…*us*…we are your family. And there isn't a damn thing my brothers, my parents, or anyone else can give her if you're not in her life."

"London—"

"She will choose you over me in a heartbeat." His eyes were blazing now, not angry—conviction burning like fire.

"That's not true," I shot back, shaking my head.

"The *hell* it isn't. She told me as much the night we started dating." He leaned in slightly, voice dropping. "*'Don't ever try to make me choose between Jones and you. You'll always lose. He's my person. Even when we get married, he'll be my person.'*"

I couldn't speak. She said that?

London straightened, arms still crossed. "Those were her words, Jones. Not mine."

He crossed the room and sank into the chair across from me. "Jones," he said quietly, his air suddenly gentler. "What is this really about?"

"I slept with Marley."

Shit.

The words tumbled out before I could shove them back down, and the second they hit the air, I wanted to swallow them whole.

"Fuckkkkkk."

London froze—then leaned back, hands shooting straight into his hair, dragging hard like he was trying to rip the thought right out of his skull. His eyes went wide, wild.

"What the fuck do you *mean*, Jones?" His voice cracked on my name. "*When?* Holy shit—"

"Yeah…" I slumped back, pressing my thumbs into my eyes, trying to breathe, trying not to puke right there on the floor. "The night before the wedding."

He went absolutely still for half a heartbeat—then erupted from the couch.

"*Three* fucking years ago, Jones?!"

The sound of it filled the apartment, sharp and echoing.

He spun in place, pacing tight circles, raking both hands through his hair like he was deciding between punching a wall or passing out cold.

"Jesus Christ," he muttered, voice half a laugh, half a growl. "She's gonna fucking kill you."

He stopped, wheeled on me, eyes blazing. "No, you know what? She's gonna fucking kill *me*. Because now *I know*. Which makes me an accomplice to this bullshit." He groaned, tugging harder at his hair. "Fuck. She's gonna kill both of us."

"I know." My voice was wrecked, small. It felt like it scraped my throat raw just saying it. "I know, London."

I stared at the ceiling, waiting for the verdict. Waiting for him to walk out. Waiting for the whole thing to implode.

"She can never fucking know." His voice cut through the silence like a blade. "I hate to say that, but never. Fucking *never*, Jones."

The words gutted me. My mouth moved before my brain caught up. "Because I'm not good enough for him?"

London spun, eyes wide, like I'd slapped him. "What?" He stepped closer, shaking his head hard. "Fuck no. You're one of the best damn people I know, Jones. Sev knows it. Hell, she *depends* on it. *That's* not the issue."

He started pacing again, words spilling faster now, sharper. "She's jealous of anyone in your orbit. You know that. She fucking hated Mason. She wanted to stab Stephanie with a rusty butter knife. Terrence nearly got a pot of boiling water to the face."

My lips twitched despite myself, but his eyes stopped me cold. He wasn't joking.

"Any and everyone she's *ever* seen you with has enraged her. Is it fair? Fuck no. But Marley?" His voice dropped, raw and heavy. "That would be an implosion. Because she couldn't be jealous of him. Not Marley. But she *would* be. And then—*boom*." He snapped his fingers, sharp enough to echo. "Implosion. Of her. Of you. Of everything."

The room was quiet again, his words still hanging between us like smoke, thick and impossible to breathe through.

"Don't you realize that's part of the problem here, Lon?" My voice broke, sharper than I meant. "How the fuck am I supposed to move on? Find my own person—someone to love *me*, to hold *me*, to fuck *me*—when she's got this grip on my life?"

London's jaw tightened, but I kept going, because once it started, it wouldn't stop.

"She's in everything. Every corner. Every choice. And what the hell am I supposed to do knowing she'll hate anyone I'm with? Not just hate—*actively try to scare off*." My laugh was hollow, ugly. "She doesn't even have to try that hard. One glare from Sev and poof—they're gone. And I'm left being the asshole who couldn't hold on to anyone because my best friend decided she didn't like them."

I dragged a hand down my face, exhaling hard. "How do I build a life when hers keeps swallowing mine whole?"

For once, London didn't have a quick reply. He just stood there, chest rising and falling slowly, watching me like he was seeing the cracks for the first time.

Finally, he asked, voice low but direct. "Can you ever really give yourself to anyone else fully, Jones? I see the way you love her. Hell, anyone with eyes can see it. So tell me—do you want to be with Marley? I know there's a flirtation there. But was that what it was? Or was it just sex for you?"

The question hit like a gut punch. My chest tightened, air burning in my lungs.

"No. I don't want to be with Marley." The words came out rough, final. "I was attracted to him, yeah, but not in a forever way. Not in a *life-long, let's have babies together* way. That's why it stayed playful, harmless… until it wasn't. We were drunk. We were lonely. And it crossed a line I wish it hadn't."

I rubbed my face, hating the sting of it, the finality in saying it out loud. It felt like closing a chapter I hadn't even realized I'd left open.

"And the truth? I know I'll never be able to give anyone all of me. Not when she's already got most of me, whether she knows it or not." A bitter laugh slipped out before I could stop it. "But I have to fucking try. What's the alternative here, man? I just… orbit her forever until I rot?"

I leaned back on the couch, staring at the ceiling, throat raw. "I've got an interview in Houston next week. Head chef position. They reached out. I didn't even go looking."

I dropped my gaze back to him, steady despite the ache

clawing at me. "I have to start making plans to live my own life, London. Or else I'm just going to die here—half man, half best friend, stuck in the middle of her world with no place of my own."

"Fucking hell, Jones." He dragged a hand down his face, the weight of it showing in his shoulders. "Yeah. I get it. I do." His voice cracked just enough to show it wasn't easy for him either.

He paced a slow line across my apartment, then stopped, pinning me with that same hard stare. "And fuck, it's selfish of me to want you to just… stay in it. To orbit her. To do anything other than this, just so she stays happy. That's on me."

I looked at him, surprise tugging at me, but he pressed on.

"You've got to tell her, though. Not about Marley—that stays buried. But the job. The possibility. If it's even a thought in your head that you might take it, Sev needs to know. And soon."

London's voice was steady, but there was steel under it. "If this is for you, don't let her talk you out of it. Do what you need to do for *you*. I promise I'll take care of her. But Jones…" His jaw flexed, eyes locking hard on mine. "Don't do it because you feel like you don't have a place here. Because you do. You *always* do. You're not some add-on, you're family. Ours. Hers." His jaw twitched. "And mine."

I let out a shaky breath. "She's gonna take it as a betrayal. Like I'm leaving *her*."

"Maybe," he admitted. "But better she hears it from you than finds out secondhand, when you're already halfway gone." He shook his head. "I won't say anything. That's not my place. You'll decide when the time's right to tell her if you decide to go."

The air between us shifted then—not lighter, not healed. Just… clearer. Like the storm had finally blown through and left wreckage scattered across the floor. This discussion didn't fix or tie anything up, but at least it's out there now.

London pushed off the counter, dragging in a slow breath that seemed to deflate everything sharp between us. "Come back to the house," he said finally. "She's freaking out. We'll deal with this storm another day."

I swallowed hard and nodded once. No fight left in me. Just the inevitability of walking back into her orbit, pretending for a little while longer that the world wasn't about to crack in half.

He stepped forward before I could say anything and pulled me into a hug. One arm hooked tight around my waist, the other braced on the back of my head.

That's the thing I love about London—he doesn't have a single ounce of performative masculinity or homophobia in him. He'll hug me like this, solid and unflinching, until I'm the one who lets go. No awkward pats or hesitation.

And fuck, I needed that.

I patted his back, blinking hard against the burn behind my eyes. "Let's get this gauntlet over with," I muttered into his shoulder.

He let out a short laugh and patted the back of my head. "I love you, Edward."

"London?"

"Yeah?" he said, still holding on.

"You make me…*feel* things when you say my name like

that."

His laugh this time was louder, shaking through both of us as he pushed me back by the chest. "Motherfucker," he said, grinning, head shaking. "Let's go."

London didn't trust me not to pull a U-turn and vanish, so I rode back with him.

You'd think it would've been awkward—two men carrying a grenade between us—but it wasn't. That's the thing about me and London: somewhere in the last three years, we've gotten close. Closer than I ever thought possible, considering how we met.

I guess you have to be when you let your wife kiss, sit on, and say the things to your best friend that Sev says to me.

So instead of detonating the silence, we talked about wedding stuff. He admitted he was actually looking forward to a week of family chaos, the kind that rattles windows and fills the house with noise—just like Simone and Derrick's wedding week. The house he designed? Built for that. Built for late nights, yelling at the TV, too many bottles of wine, Sev screaming at refs right along with his brothers. He'd planned the whole circus because he wanted to give her the wedding she never got the first time around.

Derrick and I helped him plan it down to the wire. Tried to get Marley to weigh in, but he'd been mostly MIA. Simone and Sloane handled the "girly" details, though truth be told, Sev's never really been a girly-girl. She has her moments, sure, but she's always carried that sharp, masculine energy—grit, muscle, beer in hand, voice raised over the game with the boys.

Sexy as hell. Always has been.

When we pulled up to the house, London killed the engine and just looked at me for a moment. Making sure I was steady before walking into the fire.

I knew why. Because on the other side of that door was a hurricane with my name on it.

"You okay?" he asked gently. "This isn't going to be an easy one."

"I know," I said, trying to sound braver than I felt. "We'll get through it."

And sure enough—

Hurricane.

The second she saw me, she started crying. Full-body crying, tears streaming as she barreled toward me like she was powered by rage and relief at the same time. London, the bastard, stepped neatly aside like, *you're on your own, pal.*

She grabbed my hand hard enough to leave marks and dragged me into one of the downstairs rooms, slamming the door shut behind us.

Her chest was heaving, cheeks wet, eyes blazing as she rounded on me.

Her voice cracked on my name—part fury, part heartbreak.

"Please don't cry, Sev." My voice broke, soft. I lifted her into my arms, burying her against me like I could shield her from her own storm. "I'm sorry for disappearing. I never want to be the cause of these." My thumb brushed her tears away, then I kissed her—gentle, desperate—lifting her into my arms until her legs wrapped around me. "I'm sorry, Sev. I'm so fucking sorry."

"Then why are you mad at me?"

"I'm not mad at you."

Her eyes searched mine, wounded. "You said I was being too much."

I carried her to the bed, sat down with her perched in my lap, brushing her curls back from her face. God, she's so beautiful.

"It's starting to feel like we're in this throuple, Sev," I said finally, the truth dragging itself out of me. "I get to have you like this—holding you, kissing you. And it's not just a grounding thing anymore. It's any time of day. You just hop into my lap, and even now… if someone sees us like this, outside of this house, outside of the bubble we've made? They'd think we're together."

Her lips parted, eyes shining, but she didn't speak.

"But…" My throat worked around the word. "But you go home to him. You go to his bed. His arms. After you've kissed me, curled into me, had this intimacy with me. And it's not jealousy—I swear to God it's not. You *know* me, Sev."

Her lashes trembled.

"But you've pushed out every person I've tried to bring in. Purposefully. *Vengefully*. You hated Mason. You wanted to rip

Stephanie's throat out. Terrence? You nearly poured boiling water on him." I let out a rough laugh, but there was no humor in it. "Anyone who tries to get close to me—close enough to threaten this between us—you drive them away. And I've let you. Because it's *you*."

The tears in her eyes swelled, and I knew I'd just shoved us both out of the safe, messy little orbit we'd been pretending was enough.

"You're seeing someone?" she asked, and it was more sob than question—like the words had clawed their way out of her throat against her will.

My chest clenched. God, the sound of it nearly broke me.

"No." I cupped her face, forced her to look at me. "No, Sev. I'm not seeing anyone."

Her breath hitched, eyes searching mine like she wanted to believe it but couldn't trust herself to.

"I tried," I admitted, voice rough. "I tried to let someone else in, but it never stuck. Not because of them, Sev. Because of you. You've got so much of me, there's nothing left for anyone else. You know that."

She shook her head, curls brushing my cheek as fresh tears spilled. "I don't want you to need someone else," she whispered, and it sounded like a confession and a curse all at once.

"I can't keep going like this, Sev." My voice quivered, but I anchored it. "That night—when you signed your divorce papers—something started between us. And it's been inching closer and closer to inappropriate ever since."

Her eyes widened, lips parting like she wanted to protest,

but I pushed through.

"Yeah, London's okay with it. He's been more than okay with it. But whoever I end up with someday? They won't be. They can't be."

Her tears spilled faster, her head shaking, but I kept brushing her curls back, desperate to make her see.

"I love this version of us, Sev. Christ, I do. It's been everything. It's who we are. But I need…" I swallowed hard, throat tight. "I need to start having a life outside of this. Outside of us."

Her breath hitched.

"The only way to do that is to create some physical distance," I said softly, pressing my forehead to hers. "Can you understand that? Please, Sev. Tell me you understand."

For half a second, she just stared at me, eyes wet, breath trembling against my skin.

Then her lips crashed into mine. Wet, frantic kisses, her tears salt on my tongue as she clutched at me like I was already slipping away.

"Sev—" I tried, but the next breath was stolen. Her mouth moved harder, teeth grazing, her body grinding into mine until the room tilted and the air turned molten.

"Please," she begged into my mouth, the word breaking apart.

My cock stirred against her hips, traitor that it was, and she moaned at the feel of it, desperate. Her hands fumbled at my belt.

I jerked back, catching her wrists. My chest heaved. "What

are you doing, Sev?"

Her eyes—wild, tear-shined, so damn beautiful—met mine. "I can be that for you," she whispered. "If this is what you need. Please. I can't lose you."

My throat closed up, the weight of her words hitting harder than any kiss, any plea, ever could.

"You're not losing me, Sev." I kissed her fingertips.

Her lips trembled. "Do you not want me?"

I shut my eyes, dragged in a ragged breath. "I've wanted you since the day I laid eyes on you, Sev." I let go of her hands and cupped her face, thumb trembling against her damp skin. "But you're not mine. You weren't then. You aren't now."

The silence between us stretched, unbearable, her breath ghosting against my mouth.

"The problem," I whispered, forehead pressing to hers, "is that if I keep going like this… I'll always be *yours*. No matter whose bed you sleep in. No matter whose ring you wear. You'll always own me. And I don't know if I can survive that anymore."

Her sob tore through the room, soft but violent, her body shaking against mine like I'd ripped something straight out of her chest.

"I love you, Sev." The words slipped out before I could choke them back, raw and jagged.

Her reply came just as broken. "I love you."

For a second, the air between us stilled—like maybe that was enough, like maybe saying it out loud would fix the cracks we'd been taping over for years.

But I couldn't lie to her anymore. Not even with silence.

"I have an interview next week," I said. "In Houston. Head Chef. They headhunted me, Sev. And I told them I'd at least hear them out."

Her whole body stiffened. "What?"

She pulled back from my grip like I'd burned her, hands pressing against my chest until the space yawned between us. Her face crumpled in real time, horror and disbelief colliding.

"Wha—you… you're leaving Raleigh?"

"I don't know yet," I said quickly, reaching for her, the words tumbling out in a rush. "I just need… I need—"

"To get as far away from me as possible." The way she spit it out—like venom, like surrender—gutted me.

"No. *No*, Sev. That's not—"

But she was already moving, spinning off my lap, storming for the door with her tears still wet on my shirt.

"Sev—" I bolted to my feet, emotions roaring in my chest. In three strides, I caught her, palm flat against the door before she could rip it open.

"No. Stop, Sev." I was panicking. "Don't walk out like this. Don't do that to us."

Her shoulders trembled under my hands, every line of her body taut with anger and heartbreak. She wouldn't even look at me.

"What do you want from this? From me?" My anger rose despite myself. "Do you want me to just stay here for you? Never leave? Never be with anyone else?"

"Yes!" she screamed, the sound ripping from her chest. "Yes, Jones. That's what I fucking want. I know it's selfish, I know it. But I can't help it—I don't want you with anyone else. You haven't asked me for more, and God, I'd give you more if you asked it. But no, I don't want you with anyone else."

Her words seared into me. My heart pounded like it was trying to claw its way out.

"What does that mean for me, Sev?" I demanded. "Celibacy? Never getting married, never having kids of my own? Is that really what you're asking me?"

She faltered, chest heaving, fists curling at her sides. "No, that's not… it's not—"

"It is. That's what you're asking of me. If I stay right where I am, I give up a life with someone else. I give up a future with someone else."

Her eyes snapped to mine, wet and wide, but I pushed through the ache clawing at my throat.

"I'll do it," I whispered, deadly serious. "If you ask it of me, I will. But say it, Sev. Look me in the eye and tell me that's what you want for me. And I'll drop this conversation right now, and we'll go back to the way it always was."

"You can't put that on me, Jones!"

"But it *is*. It is on you, Sev. And you need to understand what you're asking me to sacrifice."

Her voice broke, then rose sharp. "You promised me you'd never leave me."

"I'm not leaving you, Sev. That's not what this is." My voice was rising too, no matter how much I hated it.

"You *are* leaving me, Jones! You can't just put a pretty bow on moving a thousand miles away and pretend it's not!"

"Bloody hell, Sev, you're being so fucking dramatic. It's a three-hour flight. I'll still be around, goddammit—"

"Don't you dare call me dramatic!" she snapped, yanking the door open so hard it slammed into the wall with a crack. "And don't fucking follow me, Jones!"

"I'm not following you," I shouted after her, chest heaving, anger and heartbreak burning in my throat. "I'm *fucking leaving!*"

The front door rattled on its hinges as I slammed it behind me.

That's when it hit me. I didn't drive here.

"GODDAMMIT!" I roared at the night, fists clenched, throat raw.

Derrick burst out onto the porch, half-buttoned shirt, phone in one hand, blocking me on the steps like he could physically stop the implosion. His eyes were wide and unnerved, scanning the yard like the answer might be out there somewhere.

"It's fine." The words came out too blunt, my fists clenching and unclenching at my sides like I could physically hold myself together.

"It's not fucking fine, Jones. I've never—*ever*—seen you and Mom like this."

I dragged both hands through my hair, pacing hard, every nerve frayed. And then it spilled out before I could stop it.

"I have a job interview in Houston."

"Oh... oh, fuck." He dragged a hand down his face, shoulders slumping under the weight of it. "She's not gonna be okay with you gone, man. You realize that, right?"

"I just need a minute, Ricky. Please."

He stared at me for a long beat, torn between pressing and protecting. Then he just nodded, slow and quiet.

"Yeah," he said softly. "Okay. Take your minute, man."

And when he stepped back inside, the silence swallowed me whole.

"Don't fucking follow me, Jones!"

My head snapped toward Mom's voice just as she came storming out of one of the downstairs rooms—face flushed, eyes blazing, heels hammering against the stairs like gunshots.

The whole room froze.

"I'm not following you; I'm *fucking leaving!*" Jones's voice roared back, raw and furious, followed by the front door slamming so hard the walls shook.

London bolted after Mom without a second thought. Derrick shot to his feet and tore after Jones.

The rest of us? Stuck. Like statues.

"Goddammit!!" Jones's shout ripped through the quiet from outside, ragged and sharp, seconds before Derrick yanked the door open and disappeared after him.

"What the hell is going on?" Simone asked, throwing her

hands up, eyes darting between all of us.

"Hell if I know," Joe muttered, wide-eyed. "You guys have been around more than me—what's up with that?"

"Nothing that I've seen," Marcus said, shaking his head slowly. "They're… normal. Always normal when we're here."

Normal.

Yeah, sure. If that's what we were calling it.

I sat there, frozen, every muscle tight as wire. Which way was I supposed to go? Upstairs to check on Mom? Outside to check on Jones?

The truth clawed at my chest—I wasn't really in either of their corners. Not anymore. I'd been gone too long, too wrapped up in my own shit. They'd each found their person already. She had London. He had… her.

And me? I was just standing here like an outsider in my own damn family.

The house felt hollow in the silence that followed, the echo of slammed doors still hanging in the air.

Derrick came back in a few minutes later, looking rattled, jaw tight. He rubbed the back of his neck and sank down beside Simone without a word.

"What was that?" I finally asked, because no one else seemed willing to.

"Shit between Mom and Jones," Derrick muttered. "He's got an interview for a job in Houston and she's freaking out."

"He's leaving her?"

That wasn't what I was expecting.

"He's not leaving Mom. He has an interview for a job. Even if he gets it, it's still Jones. He'll still be around."

How doesn't know how Mom feels about Jones. The deeper feelings that she didn't really share, but didn't deny earlier. Still be around? That man had been the gravity of her world since before I could remember. If he left, it wouldn't just be Houston. It would be like ripping the spine out of this family.

The room felt like it was pressing in on me, so I stood. My legs moved before my brain caught up, every step out the door already heavy with regret.

Outside, the night air was cooler, quieter—but it didn't calm me.

Jones sat on the bench overlooking the lake, elbows on his knees, head bowed like the whole world was caving in. He didn't hear me at first, too far gone in his own head. The water behind him shimmered faintly in the porch light, black and endless.

"Can we talk?"

That came out squeaky as fuck.

His head snapped around, eyes narrowing like I was the last person on earth he expected to see.

For a beat, neither of us moved. The air between us buzzed with tension, with three years of silence that suddenly felt too loud.

Then he turned back to the water, jaw tight, and gave a single nod.

I blew out a breath I didn't realize I'd been holding and lowered myself onto the bench beside him. The space between us felt dense, weighted with every word we hadn't said since the wedding.

"You know what leaving her means…"

"Yeah." He didn't look at me. "I do."

"And you're still willing to do it?"

He gave a short, humorless laugh and shook his head. "You know what's fucked up? Everyone's really worried about how this is gonna affect Sev. Not one of you—not one—has asked how the fuck it's gonna affect *me*."

He fell silent for a moment, staring hard at the water. "She has… and I don't have a fucking…" His hand curled into a fist. "For fuck's sake. I can't do this right now."

The quiet that followed was brutal. Just the lake, the dark, and everything neither of us knew how to say.

Before I could even form a response, he pushed to his feet, shoved his hands into his pockets, and started walking away.

"Jones—" I called after him, but he didn't look back.

That went well. *Yay us.*

The night swallowed his footsteps, and the sound of the lake filled the space he left behind.

But he was right. Dead right.

I was sure London had given him the same speech, word for word. We were all so damn focused on Mom—on how she'd handle losing him—that no one had stopped to consider what it was doing to *him*.

The man who's been her anchor for more than a decade. The man who's been *our* anchor, whether we admitted it or not.

And the thought of him walking away—of losing him too—hit me like a punch I never saw coming.

My phone buzzing pulled me out of the spiral. I fished it from my pocket. *Remi.*

"Hey," I said softly, trying to keep the edge out of my voice.

"What's wrong?"

"Damn. Hello to you too." I tried for mock outrage, and the quiet laugh on the other end gave my riotous heart a reprieve.

"Hello, trouble," came the reply, warm enough to melt some of the tension out of me. "Now… what's wrong?"

I pinched the bridge of my nose, staring out at the water. "Everything's kind of imploding with Jones and Mom. It's a long fucking story, but—Jones has an interview in Houston, and Mom's not taking it well. She's got feelings for him, but not in a leave-London kind of way. More like…" I sighed. "More like she wants to be poly, but I don't think she's had the courage to say it out loud yet. I just—picked up on it. Fuck. I'm rambling."

"It's okay," Remi said gently. "You're processing. But listen—this isn't something you can fix tonight. It's gonna work out, and all of you are gonna be stronger for it."

A pause, softer now. "Right now, you go handle what you need to handle, yeah?"

I nodded, even though there was no one here to see it. "Yeah."

The line went quiet for a beat—just breathing, steady and

grounding.

"What do you need, baby?"

"You…" I closed my eyes, blinking back the sting. "I fucking need you here, Remi."

"I'll come whenever you're ready. If that's now, say the word. But you haven't told them we're married yet, have you?"

I'd been trying—and failing.

"No. But I will. I promise you, I will. It's not you, baby."

"I know, Mars. I don't doubt that. You'll tell them when you can, when you're ready." A pause, soft and sure. "And when you do, I'll be right there beside you. Okay?"

I swallowed hard, voice barely a whisper. "Okay."

The call ended, but the echo of it stayed, impossible to shake. I need to fucking tell them.

The house was still buzzing with tension when I walked back in. The air felt thick, voices low and cautious, like everyone was waiting for the next door to slam.

London and Jones would handle Mom—no doubt about that—so I started working on an exit strategy.

"Anybody down for Denny's?"

Every head turned my way.

"Denny's?" Derrick frowned, eyebrows scrunching.

"Yeah." I shrugged, forcing a grin. "Let's go get some pancakes and hot chocolate—like we used to after our games. Show the Pierce crew how us Moores get it done."

A few chuckles broke through the silence. The shift was small, but I could feel the pressure in the room ease by a fraction.

I don't know how long I've been walking. It can't have been long, but by the time I rounded the corner to the house, the kids were piling into two cars and pulling away.

Guilt hit first. I felt like shit for how I handled Derrick and Marley — I need to fix that, but not yet. Sev comes first.

Fuck, I don't even know where we went wrong. One minute, we were talking — me asking if she wanted me to stay, her needing to actually say it — and the next, we were shouting.

We've never argued before. Never raised our voices. And now here I am, pacing outside her room like an idiot, realizing I've single-handedly set her wedding week on fire.

I ruined it.
I ruined *her*.

Before I could talk myself out of it, my knuckles were already on her and London's door.

"Hey," was all I managed when London opened it.

Sev was on the bed, curled under the covers, shoulders shaking with sobs that gutted me.

London slipped out, closing the door behind him so it was just us in the hall. He stared at me with a weight that pinned me to the spot.

"Whatever you need to do to fix this, Jones… do it. Do you understand what I'm telling you?"

My chest went tight. *No.* No, I don't fucking think I do.

I shook my head, slowly. "No, I don't understand what you're saying, London. You need to be radio perfectly fucking clear here."

His jaw worked, hands flexing at his sides like he was holding back a storm. Then he leaned in, and goosebumps erupted down my arms.

"Fucking hell, Jones. Whatever—and I mean *whatever the fuck* you need to do. With her. To her. In that room." His eyes locked on mine, steady and unflinching. "Do it. Fix it. You have my fucking permission. Just… make it right."

I stared at him, but he wasn't finished.

He exhaled hard, shoulders rolling back. "Look—I knew this day would come. There was no way it wouldn't. I made my peace with that a long time ago. But you have to make the decision that's right for *you*. Not her. Not us. *You*." His stare softened, just barely. "But if you—Jones—feel like there's a life here? With her. With us. With this family. Then I'm all in. No matter what that looks like."

My pulse thundered. What the fuck did he just agree to? What the fuck is happening right now?

"I think that's a bigger conversation than a hallway powwow, Lon."

"Not tonight, it's not."

His words were final. Immovable. Like a gauntlet thrown down at my feet.

"I think you need to stay, London."
The words ripped out of me before I could stop them. My throat felt raw, my pulse was hammering in my ears. "I'd—uh—I don't…" I dragged a hand down my face, forcing myself to meet his eyes. "You need to stay."

His brows shot up, surprise flickering across his face before settling into something darker—something curious.

"Stay," he repeated, like he was testing the weight of the word.

"Yeah." I swallowed hard. "Because whatever's about to happen in that room—it's not just me and her. It hasn't been *just me and her* in a long fucking time. It's you, too. It's always been you. And if I walk in there without you… I don't think I'll come back out the same."

The hallway felt too small, too charged—like the air itself had teeth.

London's jaw flexed, his stare cutting straight through me. "You sure about this, Jones?"

"No." I huffed a bitter laugh, shaking my head. "But I know I can't do this…whatever *this* is… without you."

London gave a soft nod. I pushed the door open and went in first.

She was crying so hard she didn't even register us—just

curled in on herself, body shaking.

I climbed onto the bed beside her, sliding my arms around her, pulling her against my chest. London stayed in the chair on her other side, silent, steady, a quiet anchor holding the room together.

She buried her face into me, her voice muffled, wrecked. "I'm sorry I yelled at you. I know I'm selfish. I do want you to be happy—even if it's not here with me."

"I'm sorry too, Sev." My voice cracked as I pressed my lips to her hair. "I was wrong to drop all this on you the week of your wedding. I was the one being selfish." I swallowed hard, heart pounding against her ear. "I love you. I'll always love you."

Her hands found my face; her fingers cool against my feverish skin. They didn't just touch me; they claimed me, tugging me down with a gravity I had no hope of resisting. And then her mouth was on mine.

The first thing I tasted was salt, the sharp, clean sting of both our tears. It didn't matter. Nothing mattered but the feel of her. Because this wasn't the gentle, grounding kiss we'd shared a hundred times before. This was deep and slanted, desperate—the way she kissed me only when the world fell away and London wasn't in the room. It was the kind of kiss that didn't just say 'mine'; it screamed it into the silence between our ragged breaths, a primal, wordless claim that seared through every doubt.

A low sound escaped my throat, and her fingers slid from my jaw into my hair, twisting, then dragging down to scrape nails against the sensitive skin at the back of my scalp. She knew exactly what that did to me, and the moan it tore from me was completely involuntary. When she answered with a whimper of her own against my lips—Fuck—I felt my sanity begin to unravel at the edges.

Her other hand slid down, a burning trail over the fabric of my shirt, past the desperate hitch of my waistband. Her cool fingers wrapped around my cock, and the contact was so sudden, so intense, it was a shock of pure, agonizing pleasure. I was so hard it was a dull, constant ache, and her touch threatened to shatter me completely.

"Holy shit. Sev—wait," I groaned, pulling back just enough to breathe, but she only dragged my mouth back down to hers.

"Fuck."

London's voice cut through the haze, and he sounded like he was barely restrained. The sound froze her.

And then it hit.

She hadn't known he was in the room.

Her body jolted under mine, hand tearing away from my cock like I'd burned her. She scrambled back, eyes wide, staring at London like she'd just been caught cheating.

And maybe, in her mind, that's exactly what it was.

If she'd been taking us there thinking London wasn't watching, then realizing he was—she'd just crossed a line she couldn't uncross. She was seconds from falling apart.

But then London spoke with a growl that vibrated through the air and through *me*.

"Don't stop."

Sev's breath caught, sudden and startled.

"Don't fucking stop," he repeated, and the world seemed to tilt with the weight of it.

The command in his tone pinned us both where we were. Every muscle in my body went tight, heart pounding so hard it felt like it might crack a rib.

Sev froze beneath me, trembling, lips parted in disbelief, eyes flicking between me and him.

I should've pulled away. Should've given her a breath, a heartbeat, a chance to catch up to what was happening. But with London's words still hanging in the air—heavy, absolute—all I could think was: *what the hell does this mean for us now?*

"Take her top off, Edward."

Give me a minute. Holy shit.

Holy. *Fucking.* Shit.

My gaze snapped to Sev, searching. Her eyes were glassy, wide, her chest rising and falling so fast I thought she might shatter under it.

But she didn't say no. She didn't move.

She just stayed there—trembling, caught between fear and something else entirely—waiting.

My hands shook as I reached for the hem of her hoodie, tugging it upward. She let me, lifting her arms until it was gone, tossed to the side. No bra beneath—just her, bare and beautiful, tits heaving under the weight of all three of us. Nipples perfect pink buds.

I swallowed hard, my heart pounding in my chest. I looked at London, then back at Sevynn, my mind racing.

London's voice came again, low and deliberate, dragging her gaze to him, dragging me right with it.

"Do you want him to touch your tits, Sev?" London asked softly.

She nodded, trembling.

"Use your words, baby."

Her breath hitched. "Yes...I want him to touch me."

A slow, possessive smile spread across his face. His eyes, dark and intent, found mine. "Edward... use your mouth."

Fuck. My cock couldn't be harder if I tried. And the way he keeps using my real name—feels like he's pulling me into a scene, like I'd just stepped across a line I could never uncross. Being directed by London Pierce. This side of him— authoritative, unflinching, commanding—fuck, I'll never recover. I'll never walk away after this. Maybe they knew that. Maybe *he* knew. One taste and I'm gone for.

I dropped my mouth to her breast, tongue circling, teasing, flicking her nipple until it peaked under my touch. She gasped, back arching, nails dragging across my scalp. When I caught the bud between my teeth and tugged, she let out a sharp, broken moan that went straight to my cock. My hand slid beneath her other breast, fingers splayed wide, kneading, owning, while my mouth devoured the first.

"Good," London growled. "Now slide your hand down her shorts."

My head snapped up, chest heaving, her wide eyes darting between us.

His voice was darker this time, all command.

"See how wet our girl is."

Our. Fucking. Girl.

The words detonated inside me, claiming me as much as they claimed her. I felt it ripple through her too—the way her breath hitched, shuddering, like the ground had just shifted under her.

This was it. What she needed. What she craved. Three parts of a whole. We were her lifeline.

I obeyed, sliding my fingers down the soft heat of her slit, parting her, finding her slick and aching. My head dropped to her shoulder, breath ragged against her skin.

"Goddamn, Sev…"

Her nails bit into my back.

"Is she wet, Edward?"

I swallowed, fingers gliding deeper, coming away drenched. "Fucking soaked."

Sev whimpered, hips twitching, panting like every nerve in her body was fire.

"Take off her shorts and panties," London ordered, steady as a goddamn general. "Spread her open."

My pulse hammered in my throat. My movements were measured as I slid them down her hips, catching the waistband of her shorts with trembling fingers. She lifted for me without a word—automatic, trusting, needy. The little sound she made when the fabric brushed down her thighs wrecked me, guttural and wet like a plea she couldn't put into words.

I dragged them slow, agonizingly and purposefully slow, peeling the denim down over her ass, down her legs, baring inch by aching inch. The air hit her skin, and she shivered, thighs pressing together like she could shield herself from the weight of both our stares.

"Don't hide from us," London growled, and she froze, chest rising heavy.

Her panties followed, soft fabric sliding from her hips to her knees, then pooling at her ankles. She whimpered as I helped her step free, my knuckles grazing the inside of her calves.

When she was bare before us, she curled instinctively, thighs snapping together again.

"Sev." I eased my palms over her knees, slow and steady, coaxing them apart.

She resisted for one long, trembling second… then yielded.

Her thighs fell open, her slick heat glistening in the low light. My cock twitched violently, a groan torn from my chest.

"That's it. Show us how ready you are, baby. Slide a finger inside, get it nice and wet… then bring it to me, Edward."

I froze. My brain just… short-circuited.

I'm sorry, what the good garden *fuck* did he just say?

Every instinct screamed I should question it, should stop, should do *something*. But my body betrayed me—because my cock pulsed so hard I saw stars, and my hand was already moving.

Submissiveness. That's what it was. Pure, unfiltered obedience that I didn't even know I had in me until this second. His dominance locked me down, turned me inside out, and I'd obey every fucking command that came out of his mouth.

Sev's eyes snapped wide at the command, lips parting, chest heaving, but she didn't say no. She didn't pull back. She spread her legs wider.

"Fuck…" I muttered, breathless. My fingers slid over her slick folds, parting them, dipping inside. She gasped, back arching, nails digging into my arm.

I pumped slowly, once, twice, then curled just enough to feel her clench around me. Wet heat coated my fingers, dripping down my knuckles.

And then I realized what came next. London didn't look away. His eyes burned into mine, steady, unflinching. Waiting. My chest rioted with panic and need, every nerve screaming at once.

Holy fuck. He really expects me to…

I pulled my fingers free, shining with her arousal, and for a split second just stared down at them, my entire world tilting sideways.

I stood from the bed and went over to him. He didn't blink. Didn't waver. His stare was almost predatory, but still patient.

"Slide them in my mouth, Edward. Be a good boy for me."

My brain fried. Completely fried. What the fuck?

But my cock betrayed me again, jerking so hard against my zipper I thought I'd come in my pants. I couldn't breathe. Couldn't think. All I could feel was the leash in his tone, the command threading through me until there was nothing left but obedience.

"London…" I whispered.

Sev was panting behind us, pupils blown wide, chest heaving like she couldn't get enough air. But she didn't stop me. She licked her lips like she wanted to see me do it.

"Now," London rasped, leaning forward just enough for his mouth to part. "Don't make me ask again."

I trembled as I lifted my hand, my breath ragged. My fingers hovered at his lips, and then he closed his mouth over them.

Heat and tongue and dominance all at once—sucking her taste from my skin while his eyes locked on mine. A whimper tore out of me, inarticulate and helpless.

"Good boy," he murmured around my fingers before releasing them with a wet pop.

I was gone. Completely gone.

"Go back and do the same thing again. This time, with your tongue. Then bring it back to me."

My stomach dropped. My pulse roared in my ears. I'm panicking. I'm fucking panicking. Am I sweating? It's so damn hot in this room, my skin feels like it's on fire.

But my body moved anyway. Submission threading through me like a second heartbeat.

I climbed back onto the bed. Sev's eyes locked on mine. She was practically on the verge of coming just from watching all of this unfold.

Same, bitch. Same.

I pressed a kiss to her inner thigh, then the other, my lips dragging heat over her skin. She shivered, her breath catching. Another kiss higher, then another, teasing, tormenting.

Finally, I dragged one long, lingering lick up her pussy. Slow. Deliberate. Curving my tongue, collecting every drop of her arousal that I could.

"Oh god…oh…oh *ffffuuuuck*." She moaned, a desperate, broken sound that almost undid me.

"Bring it to me, Edward."

My whole body shuddered. My cock throbbed painfully in my jeans. But I lifted my head, her taste still wet on my tongue and turned toward him.

"Don't swallow it."

The command snapped through me like a whip. My tongue burned with the taste of her as I pushed to my feet, every step toward him heavier than the last.

When I stopped in front of him, his hands were already reaching. Not for me. For my belt.

His eyes never left mine as he worked it open. My breath caught. My heart—if it was still beating—had to be ready to rip out of my chest.

Leather slipped, buckle clinked, and then my pants and boxers were shoved down. My cock jutted out, flushed, straining, standing right there—inches from his face.

I had to be dead. No way I was still alive through this.

"Spit it into my mouth." His voice was low and so fucking filthy as his hand wrapped around my cock.

I jolted forward with the touch, one hand shooting out to clutch his shoulder like it was the only thing keeping me upright. My body screamed to swallow, to breathe, to do something—but I held it, Sev's taste coating my tongue.

He opened his mouth. Waiting.

My hands shook as I cupped his face, tilted it up to me. Then—God help me—I spit into his mouth. His lips closed, his throat worked as he took it, savoring it. His eyes fluttered shut. A sound left him—something between a groan and a cry.

"You taste like heaven, baby."

Sev's fingers were moving fast, slick sounds filling the air as she writhed on the bed. Her head tipped back, lips parted, eyes hazy with lust. She couldn't stop, even as London's voice sliced through the haze.

"Edward." He turned me by the hips until I was facing her. Her hand still worked between her thighs, shameless and frantic. "Did you hear me tell our girl she could touch her pussy?"

My lungs burned. His hand was still on my cock, stroking slow, then rough, dragging me right to the edge of breaking, then slowing. I wanted to answer, but all that came out was a ragged gasp. I shook my head.

"Use your words, Edward." His fist tightened around me, his strokes getting harder. "Tell me."

"No." I moaned. "No, you didn't."

Sev whimpered, caught between guilt and desperate need, fingers still circling her clit like she couldn't stop even if she wanted to.

London's gaze flicked to her, then back to me. His mouth curled into something that looked too close to a dare.

"Sev, bend over the bed. In front of Edward."

Her eyes shot to his, wide, trembling, but her body obeyed

before her brain caught up. She slid to the edge, chest sinking into the mattress, ass high.

"You're going to spank her now," London said, pumping me harder, his words leaving no room for escape. "Aren't you, Edward?"

"Fuck…" The word tore out of me, helpless, because my cock was throbbing in his grip, my head was spinning, and she was right there waiting for me.

"Aren't you, Edward?" His voice sharpened, relentless, each word synced to the merciless stroke of his hand.

"Yes." I couldn't breathe. "Yes, I'm going to spank her."

London's grip loosened, then released, leaving me swaying like his hand had been the only thing anchoring me. "Spank her good," he growled, leaning back, "and then, I'll let you both come."

I nearly buckled. My cock throbbed, aching from the loss of his touch, my whole body trembling as his next words dropped like a gavel:

"Three. Count them down, baby."

Sev's arms braced against the bed, ass lifted, body quivering like she already knew how much this would undo her.

I stepped in behind her, pressing my cock to the curve of her ass. *Fuck,* she's beautiful like this—arched, waiting, mine. My palm skimmed over her right cheek, slow at first. Then I drew back and let it land. A sharp crack echoed as my hand met her skin—clean, deliberate, *perfect.*

"One," she gasped, breath shuddering, thighs clenching tight. Her ass arched higher, offering itself—*begging* for more.

My cock jerked so hard I nearly lost it.

London's voice came low and thick with approval. "Mmm. Good fucking boy."

Crack.

Her body jolted, a raw whimper spilling into the sheets.

"F-fuck… two." Her hips rolled against the bed, desperate, chasing friction, chasing anything.

I barely raised my hand for the third when London's fingers wrapped around my cock again, stealing every breath from my lungs.
He smeared the slick at my tip with his finger, and my knees buckled.

Then he stepped past me, toward Sev—like a king surveying what's his.

"Open, baby." His voice softened into something coaxing—*dark silk over steel*. "See what you're doing to our boy."

Sev lifted her head, hair wild around her face, lips parted as she turned toward him and took his finger into her mouth, tasting me. Her voice trembled, and it shot straight through me.

"Oh my God…" she whispered, her eyes locking on mine—on the sight of London's hand wrapped around my cock, stroking slow, shameless.

"Last one, sweetheart," London said, low and charged.

Sev whimpered, her body sinking into the sheets at the promise, legs trembling.

Then London's eyes snapped to me—dark, unwavering,

commanding.

"Make this one count, baby."

My chest seized. *Fuck.* That word in his voice—possessive, electric—had my cock twitching in his grip before I even moved.

I stepped in close, hand trembling as I ran it over Sev's perfect ass. She was breathless, her whole body strung tight, waiting.

And then—

Crack.

The sound cracked through the room like a whip, the sting blooming red against her skin.

Her cry broke, raw and sweet, spilling into the mattress. "Three..."

And just like that, she melted — thighs parting, hips rocking, her pussy glistening and begging for more.

"Good boy," London rasped, stroking me harder, his approval curling low in my gut, winding me tighter. "Look at her. Look what you've done to our girl."

Her body was trembling, hips grinding into the bed, begging without words. London's grip on my cock tightened, slick with my precum, his voice a low growl in my ear.

"Now, Edward. Slide that perfect pierced cock into her. Don't hold back."

I didn't. I couldn't if I tried.

One thrust—hard, deep—burying myself to the hilt.

The sound that tore from Sev's throat was ragged, *shattered,* desperate.

"Are you okay?" I asked, holding still by sheer force of will. No matter how wet she was, I'm still fucking huge—and with the piercings, I should've eased in.

"I'm fucking perfect. I need more, Jones. *Please.*"

I slid almost all the way out, then slammed back in.

"Fuck!" I snarled, fingers digging into her hips like they were the only thing keeping me from unraveling. The heat, the grip of her cunt—tight, dripping, perfect—*too* perfect.

I was hanging on by a thread.

"Don't you dare stop until she comes."

"Yes sir." I breathed, and I could hear the way those two words nearly pushed him over the edge.

I started rutting into her. Each thrust harder than the last, driving her forward against the mattress. She was keening, broken moans spilling out, her fists clutching the sheets as she tried to push back, meet me stroke for stroke.

Her body quaked, shuddering beneath me, her pussy clenching so tight around my cock it nearly ripped my control to shreds.

"Come for him, baby," London coaxed, voice thick with heat. The sound of his fist working his cock—slick, relentless— was almost too much. "Show him how fucking good you are for us."

And she *shattered.*

Her scream tore through the room as her body convulsed, wet and pulsing around me, dragging me straight over the fucking edge with her.

My hips stuttered, losing rhythm, lost to her.

Then London's hands were on me—yanking me back by the waist, just before I could collapse. He dropped into the chair behind him, calm and in control, pulling me to stand between his legs.

My cock jutted forward—hard, leaking, flushed—still pointed right at Sev.

"Come here, sweetheart," he ordered, voice thick. "Edward needs to come. Did those piercings feel good in your pussy, baby?"

"Yes. Fuck. Yes."

Her legs shook as she came to kneel in front of me, right between my thighs. When her eyes lifted up to mine, it hit me—like we were seeing each other for the first time in this new reality. Nothing casual. Nothing ground-level anymore. Something dangerous. Something permanent.

"You want him to come, sweetheart?" London murmured, his hand stroking my cock—still slick with her arousal, with *us*.

Sev didn't hesitate. Her gaze stayed locked on mine. "Yes. Please."

That *please* wrecked me.

Before I could think, London's fist tightened, pumping me with ruthless precision—expert, merciless. Her eyes on me. His hand on me. Her scent thick in the air.

It was *too much*. Too fucking much.

"Open, baby," London rasped, turning his gaze to her. "He's close."

Sev's lips parted, tongue sliding out with aching anticipation—and that sight alone shattered me.

The orgasm hit like a detonation. My groan was low, guttural, animal. I came straight into her waiting mouth, her eyes never breaking from mine.

I'd never come like that before. Not once. Not with anyone. Not even alone.

Because the second she opened for me—those lips I'd kissed in a thousand harmless ways—it was *over*.
I erupted so hard I nearly folded in half, my vision going white, knees buckling like London was wringing the very soul out of me with his fist.

And Sev? *Fuck.* She *took it*. Swallowed every drop. Grabbed her tits like watching me come undone got her off just as hard as the taste. She moaned—low, guttural, filthy—as if my release was the only thing she'd ever needed in her life.

I couldn't breathe. Couldn't *think*. My heart jackhammered in my chest so violently I thought it might crack my ribs. My hands fisted in her curls, tight and desperate—just to keep myself upright, because I was *gone*.

Watching her swallow me down, her eyes locked to mine the whole fucking time?

That was it.

That was the line. And I knew—*in my bones*—I'd never walk this back.

"Good. Fucking. Girl." London's voice rolled through the room like thunder.

He stood. Tugged her up by the arm. And kissed her so hard my knees nearly gave out again—my cum still fresh on her tongue, and he devoured it like a man *starving*.

Then he turned. His gaze cut to me.

Before I could move, his hand was on my throat—rough, calloused fingers clamping down just enough to make my pulse riot beneath his grip.

My back slammed into the wall. My breath hitched hard as his eyes locked onto mine.
There was no escape—not from that stare.

"This makes you mine now," he growled, low and lethal.
The pressure tightened, just enough to tilt the room.
Heat flooded down my spine, every nerve screaming with submission and want.
"Understand?"

I nodded before I could think, a full-body shudder ripping through me—*betraying me.*
My cock twitched. My body answered before my mouth ever could.

And then—*fuck*—he kissed me.

Tentative, at first. Testing. Like he wanted to see if I'd flinch. When I didn't, it was like that was the permission he needed to deepen the kiss. His mouth claimed mine with an intensity that made my toes fucking curl. His other hand grabbed a handful of my hair at the base of my bun, tilting my head. His tongue traced mine with deliberate strokes that had me making embarrassing as hell sounds into his mouth.

When he pulled back, I was breathless, and he was calm as fuck.

His hand dropped from my throat and the world snapped back into place—too sharp and way too damn bright.

"Give each other some aftercare, and I'll be right back to tuck you both in."

And just like that, he walked off, leaving me pressed against the wall, still reeling, still burning, wondering when the hell I'd stopped being just Sev's—and become his too.

The bathroom door clicked shut behind him. Steam already beginning to hum through the crack.

Sev and I just... stared. Like we were strangers in a brand-new world, neither of us had a map for.

The laugh clawed its way out of my throat before I could stop it—half hysterical, half holy-shit-I'm-ruined. "What... and I mean this with all sincerity... the fuck just happened, bitch?"

Her chest hitched, then she was laughing too. Wet, shaky, broken laughter that tangled with tears. She pressed her hand over her mouth like she was trying to muffle it, but her eyes were wide and wild.

"We—" she choked out, shaking her head. "We just..." She couldn't even finish. Just buried her face in her hands and laughed harder.

"Yeah," I muttered, dragging a hand through my hair, still trembling. "We just."

Sev dropped her hands, eyes locking on mine, and before I could smirk or backpedal, she was right there—close, heat radiating off her. Her mouth found mine, desperate and sweet all at once.

The laugh died in my throat, swallowed up by her kiss.

We were still naked, raw and undone. I lifted her easily, her legs winding around my waist like they'd been waiting there all along. Her arms looped around my neck, her tongue teasing against mine as the kiss deepened, until it was less about lips and more about tasting each other whole.

No rush. No command. No audience. Just us.

Her hands were in my hair, tugging, exploring, mapping me like I was brand-new. My palms slid down her back, memorizing the slope of her spine, the arch of her hips. I pressed her tighter to me, groaning into her mouth when her body rocked against mine, slow and hungry.

For once, we weren't grounding each other. We weren't pretending. We were just… kissing. Deeply. Recklessly. Like two people trying to memorize what it felt like to finally stop holding back.

With her still in my arms, I shifted, lining up and pushing into her slow. Inch by inch. Her head tipped back, lips parted, but no sound came out, just a broken shudder of breath as I filled her.

I lifted her, then dropped her down again until I was buried to the hilt, her heat gripping me so tight it nearly buckled my knees.

"Fuck, Sev…" My mouth found her neck, my voice a rough rasp against her skin. "I'll never get over how good you feel wrapped around my cock. It's… *fuck*, it's more than I ever thought it would be. Heaven."

Her nails scraped into my shoulders as I kissed her, rutting into her now, the pace quickening, the thrusts going deeper, harder. She buried her face into my shoulder, muffling the moan that ripped through her throat.

I groaned, clutching her tighter, slamming her down onto

me with every stroke, chasing that sharp edge between possession and worship.

"I'm yours, Jones." She breathed it out like a vow, her body trembling under mine. "Oh god… fuck, I'm gonna come—"

I carried her to bed without breaking rhythm, laying her back and hiking her legs over my shoulders. Then I drove into her, pistoning deep, swallowing every one of her moans with my mouth.

"Fuck… your piercings, Jones. Fuuuck—oh god!"

She shattered, crying out, her body clenching so hard around me I nearly blacked out. Wet heat gushed over me, spilling down my thighs, and my brain short-circuited because holy fuck—Sev was gushing like a fountain, soaking me, the sheets, everything.

"Fuck, Sev—goddamn." I tore myself free, hand wrapping around my cock, stroking hard as I watched her unravel beneath me. Watching her shake, watching her flood the bed with every aftershock—it was the filthiest, most beautiful fucking thing I'd ever seen.

"Holy… fuck," I choked as the edge hit me like a freight train. My body snapped forward and I came hard—thick streams painting her stomach, her breasts, marking her like I couldn't stop myself even if I tried.

Her back arched, eyes half-lidded, hands sliding up through my release, smearing it over her skin like she wanted to wear me. Claim me the same way I'd just claimed her.

And fuck if that sight didn't gut me more than the orgasm itself.

The room was ravaged. Sheets soaked, our bodies still

trembling, the air thick with sex and sweat and something I couldn't name. We just…stared at each other. Her chest rising and falling, mine still trying to catch up. Her lips parted, the faintest smirk tugging at the corner.

That smirk—it got me every damn time.

I mirrored it, slow and crooked, dragging my thumb across her cheek like I had to make sure she was real. Silence stretched between us, not awkward, but charged. Almost like we'd just redrawn the map of the world and now had to sit in it.

"I'm yours, too, Sev," I said, my voice rough as gravel, "I've always been yours."

I kissed away the tears that started to fall, kissed down her jaw. "I love you so fucking much, Jones. I need and want you no less than I need and want London. I need this, us. All of us. Marry me. Marry us."

RLM: How did the rest of last night go? You didn't call me back. Are you okay?

Fuck. How did last night go?

Mom was pissed at Jones.

Jones was pissed at all of us.

I tried to talk to him — disaster.

Then I got everyone the hell out of dodge before Jones got back, because I *knew* shit was about to hit the fan.

We ended up at Denny's till four in the fucking morning.

Now it's noon, and I'm just opening my damn eyes.

Yeah. Great fucking night. And the guilt's still gnawing at me.

> **Marley:** *Sorry. It was a shit night, and I should've called or texted. Are you okay?*

I feel like shit right now.

RLM: I'm fine. Are you okay? Do you want to talk about it?

And say what…

Marley: No.

Fuck, I'm being a dick.

Marley: Not right now. But soon. Promise.

RLM: Are you sure you're okay? You don't seem like yourself right now, Mars.

I shut my phone off and drag my hand through my hair.

I don't even know what's got me so wound up.

I just… want Remi here.

I hate that I've split my life in two—one version for them, one for us. So much of what matters doesn't include my family anymore, and none of them deserve that. Especially Remi.

Everything's changed in the last three years, and I just need to tell them. Tell them I'm married. Bring Remi home. Maybe then we could finally breathe, finally just *be*.

But it's not that simple.

I know they'll be happy for us—if nothing else, they just want me happy—but being married for a year and a half without saying a word? That's going to blow up like fireworks, and I'm trying to avoid the fallout.

Fuck. I'm spiraling.

I drag on a pair of shorts and a T-shirt, trying to shake it off, and head downstairs.

"Look who rejoined the land of the living," Sloane says, already pouring coffee. She slides a mug toward me as I take a stool at the kitchen island.

"You look like hell—and considering you're the only one of us who didn't drink last night…" Her eyebrows do the rest of the sentence for her.

"Jet lag," I lie, wrapping both hands around the mug like it might ground me.

She lets out a laugh. "You don't get jet lag from a two-hour flight from New Orleans, dipshit."

"Hey—language, young lady," London says as he strolls into the kitchen. He checks the time and lets out a low whistle. "Did everyone sleep like the dead today? Damn, I can't remember the last time I slept this late."

"Are Mom and Jones okay?" I ask.

Something flickers across his face. Quick. But even Simone catches it.

"Yeah. They're fine," he says after a beat. "They hashed it out last night."

He takes a long sip of coffee, eyes somewhere else entirely.

Simone and I trade a look. Something doesn't sit right, but I don't have the energy to push it.

"What did you all get up to last night?" he asks.

London hasn't changed much over the past three years. Barely at all, really. Sloane, though—she's filled out a little. Softer around the edges. There's a small curve to her stomach, and I noticed her pretending to drink last night. She's acting hungover now, but I'd bet money she's pregnant.

I've never looked at Simone as anything but a sister, but she's always been beautiful—thin but still curvy, all soft edges and sharp confidence. Which is why the slight curve in her abdomen is noticeable if you're paying attention.

"We ended up at Denny's until around four in the morning," she says, tugging her hair into a messy knot. "Derrick smuggled in those tiny liquor bottles, and we had pancakes and tequila. Breakfast of champions."

"Yeah," I add, taking a slow sip of coffee to hide my grin. "I was craving their sausage gravy—was gonna mix it with syrup and pour it over my steak—but they were out."

I say it casually, like it's just a terrible culinary confession. But my eyes stay on Simone out of the corner of my vision.

Her reaction is immediate—same as last night. The second the words leave my mouth, her hand shoots up to cover her mouth, eyes going wide.

Bullseye.

Remi's sister once told me that grotesque food combos could take out even the toughest pregnant stomach. Looks like she knew what she was talking about.

"Excuse me," Simone mumbles before making a beeline for the bathroom.

Two for two. Yeah—she's definitely pregnant. I'll have to apologize when they finally announce it—after I stop laughing at the fact that I made her throw up *twice*.

"I think she had the same bad eggs that I had. I was not feeling great when we got home." I lie to cover for her. They'll tell when they are ready.

"Oh, that's shit. I'm sorry, Mars. You good now?"

"Yeah. Thanks, London."

He steps closer and drops onto the stool beside me—too close.

"Marley." He sets his coffee down, voice low. "About you and Jones, and what happened after Ricky's wedding…"

I inhale sharply, and I nearly choke on my coffee.

What the *fuck?* Jones told him?

London's hand is suddenly on my back, patting between my shoulder blades while I cough up a lung.

Once I finally get a breath, I wipe my mouth with the back of my hand and rasp, "He told you?"

London just nods. "This is information I know *against my will*, Marley. Completely and utterly against my fucking will." He leans in a little, eyes serious now. "But your mom can never find out. Do we understand each other?"

The hell?

"I told her yesterday." My brow furrows. "Why?"

"You told her?" He looks almost panicked. "Everything go okay?"

I nod slowly. "She was shocked, yeah. But we talked it through, and she knows it was a stupid, drunken mistake. It needed to be said. Now things can… I don't know. Be okay again."

Something shifts in London's expression. His eyes widen like a lightbulb just went off.

"Is that why, Marley?" He grabs my shoulder, grip tightening. "Is that why you haven't been home?"

Fuck.

I don't want to do this. Not now.

I need Remi.

"Yeah…" I shake my head. "Yeah. I just couldn't really face anyone after that. I was…" Spit it out, damnit. "I was ashamed of what I did and with who I did it with and I decided to take a few weeks to shake it off. Those weeks turned into months. Then years." I raise my hands in defeat. "Now, here we are."

"Do you have feelings…for…?"

"No…no. It's not that. I'm marr…" Fuck. This is too much. "I'm mad at myself for what I did and for waiting so long to make it right."

Coward. I could've just said it. Finished the sentence.

"I'm sorry you felt this way all this time, Marley. You're right. I'm glad you told her."

I nod. I don't fucking know what to do anymore.

"What are we so dumpy about?" Derrick mumbles as he shuffles into the kitchen, wearing nothing but a pair of athletic shorts.

"Don't you own a shirt, fucker?" I shoot back, half-laughing as I give London one last nod.

"Look, you beefcake Barbie, fuck off. I like being shirtless," Derrick groans, reaching for the coffee pot. He pours himself a cup, takes one sip, and grimaces. "Ugh. This coffee's shit. Who made it?"

"That would be your wife—and mother of your future children—right there, Derrick," I say smugly, watching his eyes widen as they flick between me and London. "You know, whenever you two decide to bring a few gremlins into the world and feed them after midnight." I grin into my mug.

He laughs, but it sounds borrowed. "Yeah." A hollow chuckle. "Yeah, years… years from now."

He glances at London, nervous, but London isn't even looking at him.

Because Mom and Jones just walked into the kitchen — and something in London's face shifts.

Something's off.

Goddammit, London. Play it cool.

Sev and I round the corner into the kitchen, and there he is—watching us like we're his last meal and he hasn't eaten in days. Heat crawls slow and traitorous down my spine. My neck's damp. My pulse is a traitor too.

Last night was…

Christ.

Last night was the best thing that's ever happened to me, and my body still hasn't recovered. I feel loose, warm, and thoroughly, beautifully ruined in all the right places. Finally having Sev like that—really having her—was… revelatory. Like stepping out of grayscale and suddenly remembering the world is made of color and breath and wanting.

I woke tangled in her this morning, her thigh hooked over mine, her skin hot and soft and familiar in a way that felt ancient—even if we've barely begun. And London was already gone, because of course he was. Because if he'd stayed, none of us would've left the bedroom today.

She asked me to marry them last night.

I didn't answer. Didn't know how. Didn't know if she meant it or if it was just bliss talking, her mind still floating somewhere between earth and the place she dragged me. I don't even know how any of that works legally, emotionally... whatever the hell this is. Poly laws? Vows? Who goes where on the paperwork? I tried to brush it off as post-orgasm delirium, especially since she fell asleep five minutes later, snoring into my throat.

But the truth? The idea lodged itself under my skin and refused to move. It hummed through me. And then London came out of the shower—forever in there, which, considering he didn't come with us... yeah. I'm not an idiot. I know what all that hot water and heavy breathing was about.

He didn't go to his side of the bed. Didn't reach for her.

He came straight to me.

Slid in close enough that I could feel the heat still clinging to him from the steam, close enough that my stomach dropped and my breath went thin.

"Turn to me, Jones," he whispered low so he wouldn't wake Sev.

Carefully, like the universe might snap if I moved too fast. My insides were doing jumping jacks, flips, *somersaults* being that close to him after everything we've been avoiding, everything we've pretended was just tension instead of truth.

When I faced him, he was already looking at me like I was something he'd been starving for. Like he finally let himself want out loud.

"Are you okay?" he asked, voice still quiet, but his eyes locked hard on mine.

"Are *you*?"

He gave me a look—equal parts amused and exasperated. "Don't answer my question with a question, Edward."

He licked his lips, glanced down, then met my eyes again. "Now. Answer me."

I swallowed, my throat dry. "I don't know. I feel... off balance."

His brow furrowed slightly, the concern slipping in. "What can we do to give you better balance?"

I let out a breath—more of a tired and uncertain laugh. "Tell me what this is. What it *means*. Was it a one-and-done? Because Sev asked me to marry you both a few minutes ago, and then fell asleep like she didn't just drop a bomb in the middle of the goddamn room. And now you're here. Half-naked. Looking at me like you want a hell of a lot more than just to *talk*, and it's making me fucking nervous."

I hesitated, then asked what I'd been holding back for weeks. "Are you... bi? Curious?"

He didn't answer. Just smirked—*bastard*.

"That's gonna take some... balancing," he said, and I wanted to punch him and kiss him in the same breath.

Then he leaned in, close enough to taste the tension on his breath. His voice was low and steady, softer now.

"How about we save the heavy stuff for when she's awake—when all of us can talk about it. And for now... you just let me kiss you."

His eyes searched mine, quietly asking something that felt far bigger than a kiss.

"Would you like that, Edward?"

I nodded. A small, shaky movement that somehow felt monumental.

The moment I did, his hand came up, cradling the back of my head. His fingers threaded through my hair, closing into a firm grip at the base of my neck—right where control lived, where surrender waited. And then he kissed me deep and hard. His mouth claimed mine like he'd earned it. Like I'd already said yes in ways I hadn't even realized. There was nothing tentative left in him now. Just hunger. Precision. A kiss that pulled the breath from my lungs and replaced it with fire.

I kissed him back.

God help me, I kissed him back with everything I had left.

I wanted to touch him. To feel every inch of him. But the moment my hand rose, the weight of Sev sleeping just behind us slammed into my chest like a warning. My thoughts spun out.

My chest tightened. My hand hovered halfway between restraint and need. What were the rules here? Should we be doing this without her? Would she be angry? Would it *hurt* her to wake up and see this? Or would it hurt her more to know I'd *wanted* it and pulled away?

Still, my body moved without asking permission from my brain. My hand slid down, tracing over the lines and ridges of London's abs—warm, taut, impossibly hard. My fingertips skimmed the waistband of his shorts…

And there he was.

His cock was already out, thick and rigid, curving up from the fabric like it had been waiting just beneath the surface for this moment. Waiting for *me.*

He inhaled sharply when I touched him—just a brush across the tip, wet and hot and aching.

"Do it," he whispered, voice strained, like even he wasn't sure how much longer he could hold back. "Now, Edward."

So, I did.

I reached inside and wrapped my hand around him. Jesus. *Jesus.*

This man was *blessed.* Thick, heavy, velvet over steel—he pulsed against my palm like he was barely holding it together.

His hips jolted forward into my grip, and a soft moan escaped his mouth—unfiltered, gorgeous.

And that's when I felt it—Sev moving behind us, stirring and shifting the sheets. I froze, guilt and panic colliding like fists in my chest. But London didn't even blink. Didn't glance away. His eyes were already locked on hers.

And when he spoke again, it wasn't a whisper.

"Don't you fucking stop," he growled. His voice was low, guttural, laced with command. "Keep going."

And before I could overthink it, I leaned down and took him into my mouth in one fluid move, swallowing him deep.

"*Ffffuckkk—*" he snarled, his head snapping back as the word ripped through gritted teeth.

Behind me, Sev's hands traced over my back, urging me on, grounding me in *all of this*. I reached up and took his other hand, guiding it to the back of my head—giving him permission. And he took it.

Both hands tangled in my hair as he began to rut into my mouth—hard, controlled, and relentless. His hips snapped forward in deep, punishing thrusts, using my mouth like it belonged to him.

"Goddamn, Edward." His voice was wrecked now. "Such a good fucking boy. Ffffuuuck."

His breath was ragged, broken into curses as he came—hot and thick, spilling over my tongue. I swallowed without hesitation, tasting salt and heat and the rawness of being *wanted* this way.

Behind me, Sev cried out.

"*God—*" she moaned, her body trembling against mine, her release catching her off-guard. I felt the shudders ripple through her, felt the electricity arc between the three of us like we'd become one circuit, closed and live.

London released my head gently, still panting as he pulled me upward, guiding my face to his. And then he kissed me. Deep. Filthy. Tender. Full of everything he hadn't said.

And before I could catch my breath, Sev was there—pulling me toward her, wrapping her hand around the back of my neck, and kissing me like she *knew* exactly what I tasted like. Like it belonged to *both* of them now.

And maybe it did. Maybe I belonged to them both now.

I didn't even need release. That moment—wrapped in their mouths, their hands, their eyes—had left me full in a way I'd never felt before. Every muscle melted. Every question quieted. Sleep pulled me under not long after, soft and slow like warm water.

I never thought I'd see the day I'd be with Sev, sexually. There were moments, sure—kisses that lingered too long, glances that said too much—but we'd always stopped short. We were careful. Controlled. And now? Now that I've been inside her, tasted her, tasted London…I can't tell if it was salvation or the worst mistake I've ever made.

"Coffee?" London's voice snaps me back. He lifts his mug, a wry twist to his mouth.

"It's made, but for the love of God, don't let Sloane near the coffee machine again. She should know better." He's still muttering when Sloane walks in—arms crossed tight over her middle, eyes locked on Marley.

Marley's smirk is pure trouble.

What the hell did we walk into?

Sev makes her rounds, giving hugs and cheek kisses. "Good morning, my loves." She coos.

"You're in a better mood," Derrick says.

Sev blushes as she pours herself a cup of coffee. "I slept really well," she says, smiling into the steam like it's keeping her secret.

I drag a hand through my hair, praying for the floor to open up and swallow me whole. I didn't think I'd feel this… *unmoored.* Not just guilty…*disoriented,* like the room tilted while I wasn't looking.

"Let's go to lunch. All of us?" Sev says brightly, waving her cup like an invitation to normalcy.

"I'd, uh…" Marley starts, tracing the rim of his mug with one finger. His voice is quiet, careful. "I'd like to cook lunch today. If that's okay?"

The room goes still. Eyes shift.

"Last night was a fluke," Derrick deadpans. "You'll burn the house down if you try that shit again."

The words hit harder than he meant them to. It's subtle, but I see it—the way the light flickers out behind Marley's eyes.

Just tell them, Marley. They'll be proud of you.

"What were you thinking of cooking, *Marley baby?*" The old nickname slips out before I can stop it. But fuck, he looks so small, I couldn't help it. "Do you have everything you need?"

That perks him up, just a little. His shoulders square, but he still scans the room—waiting, hesitant—like he's braced for someone to shut him down.

"You all know the Michelin Star Restaurants LeVeaux? Chef Marulli?" he asked, still looking down at his cup.

"Uh, yeah!" Derrick says with a mocking wave.

"Beautiful restaurants," Sev adds. "The one in Vegas is my favorite. What about them?"

His eyes dart up, searching the room before dropping again. "I… work there."

Finally.

"Doing dishes?" Derrick laughs.

"Baby boy." My tone cuts through the room, edged but low. Derrick looks over, and I shake my head, mouthing *no*.

Marley's shoulders deflate, and Sev walks over to him, rubbing his shoulder and kissing his temple. "Doing dishes is nothing to be ashamed of, baby. I met Jones when he was doing dishes, remember?"

"She's right, Mars," Sloane adds as London nods and hums in agreement.

Fuck. No one is letting him speak. They always do this to him.

"Marley." I call.

His eyes meet mine—and for a second, he's a kid again in a grown man's body.

"You don't do the dishes there… do you?" I ask, stepping closer, stopping across the island where he can't look anywhere but at me. "You're all making assumptions. Let him say what he's trying to say."

I hold his gaze, steady, patient. I can see it—some small wall inside him finally breaking.

Progress.

"I'm the Executive Chef there."

There he is…

11 | MARLEY

"I'm the Executive Chef there," I finally manage.

Of course they'd think I wash dishes. I knew exactly how this conversation would go. The only reason I'm saying it now is because the Michelin Guide Ceremony's coming up, and I want them all there. Even Jones.

The room goes quiet. Too quiet. Everyone's exchanging these weird, uncertain glances.

"That's pretty fucking amazing, Marley baby," Jones says, breaking the silence as he crosses the room to pull me into a hug.

"Executive Chef?" Mom repeats, her voice trembling.

I nod, a lump forming in my throat. For the first time in years, she actually looks *proud*.

"I, uh…" I drop my gaze and smile softly, thinking about last week. "I found out that I'm getting a Michelin Star. And I want you all to be there." I glance at Jones. "All of you."

He nods. "Proud of you, Marley baby."

"I don't even know what to say, Mars," Mom whispers, her hands pressed to her lips. "I feel like I'm in shock."

"There's a lot to catch you up on," I say, rubbing at the back of my neck. "But I wanted to start with that."

Their awe — all that wide-eyed pride — it's almost too much. I can feel myself folding inward, like I don't deserve it.

"Baby…"

Finally, Mom moves. She wraps her arms around me, and I can feel her crying into my chest. "I hate that you felt like you couldn't tell me. How long have you been there?"

"Just a few months shy of three years," I whisper. "But I've been Executive Chef for a year and a half."

She stiffens, her head shaking against me. Guilt crawls through my chest. She doesn't know me anymore. Her own son.

"I wanted to tell you when I made something of myself," I say quietly. "When there was nothing left for you to doubt or worry about. There's… more. But we can talk through the rest soon. I promise." I swallow hard. "Just…will you come to the ceremony?"

"We wouldn't fucking miss it for the world, Mars," Derrick says, and I can hear the hitch in his voice.

When I look over, Simone's hand is moving gently over the small of his back. He's turned away from us, staring up at the ceiling.

Fucking whiny bitch.

I wipe my own tears, but I'm smiling.

"What are you cooking for us?" London asks, patting my back before leaning down to kiss my temple.

I puff my chest a little as Mom steps back. "It's called *Bayou Smoke.*"

Her fist lands on my chest—not hard, more like punctuation. "Marley *fucking* Moore!" she cries. "Is that *your* creation?"

My grin spreads wider. I knew she'd recognize it. It's the restaurant's signature dish now, drawing guests from all over the world.

Derrick and the others exchange confused glances, not understanding the weight of it, but I nod anyway.

And then Mom rushes forward again, arms looping around my neck, tears spilling warm against my skin. "My God, Marley. My God."

Her voice trembles — pride, disbelief, love — all tangled together. And I let myself believe it too.

"Somebody want to fill us in?" Derrick says, blinking hard. "I feel left out, *Mother.*"

I laugh, ready to explain the dish myself, but Mom turns sharply, already taking over.

I can only smile and listen as she tells my story better than I ever could — every word laced with the kind of pride I've been starving for. The lump in my throat grows until it's nearly choking me.

"I have a snippet of an article," she says, fumbling with her phone. "I was going to use your concept as inspiration for the new restaurant. I can't believe this was you. *The whole time,* Marley."

I swipe a hand beneath my eyes, trying not to fall apart completely.

She starts reading aloud, her voice soft but steady:

*"**LeVeaux: Where Smoke, Soul, and Sophistication Collide** — New Orleans, Louisiana. In a city that already knows how to eat, LeVeaux dares to make you fall in love with food all over again. Hidden behind an unmarked wrought-iron gate in the Marigny, the restaurant hums with quiet confidence. Brick walls, candlelight, and low brass music set the tone — intimate but electric, like something sacred is about to happen.*

At the heart of it all is Executive Chef Maverick, a Louisiana native—"

She pauses, giving me a look. "You're not a Louisiana native, and why Chef Maverick."

I look over at Jones. He gives me a proud smile, placing a hand over his heart. I think I'll keep that between him and me. I duck my head, sheepish. Mom smiles faintly and keeps reading.

"—whose cooking feels like a love letter to the bayou, written in smoke, butter, and precision. Trained in classical French technique under Chef LeVeaux himself, but rooted in Southern soul, Maverick's tasting menu is both reverent and rebellious — honoring local ingredients while pushing them somewhere unexpected.

The dish everyone talks about — and photographs obsessively — is the now-iconic Bayou Smoke. When it arrives, it looks deceptively simple: a glass cloche resting over a porcelain plate. Then, with a flourish, the server lifts the dome, and a swirl of pecan-wood smoke escapes, curling through the candlelight before dissolving into the air.

Beneath it lies a composition so beautiful it almost feels wrong to touch — butter-poached lobster glistening against sweet-corn custard, finished with a delicate andouille crumble for a whisper of heat and texture. Each bite tells a story — rich, smoky, sweet, and deeply Southern — the kind of dish that lingers long after the last taste, haunting in the best way.

'Everything we do here is about balance,' Chef Maverick says, wiping his hands on his apron, eyes bright with quiet pride. 'You can't fake depth. You build it — one layer, one ingredient, one story at a time.'

And that's exactly what LeVeaux does. It doesn't shout. It doesn't rush. It seduces — slow, smoky, and unforgettable."

Mom lowers the phone, her hand trembling as she wipes her face. But no one's looking at her. They're all looking at me.

Her voice cracks when she says it — barely above a whisper. "This is *you*, baby."

Jones starts clapping first. Thunderous. Then the others join in until the whole kitchen fills with the sound — hands, laughter, tears.

Derrick and Simone wrap their arms around me. Mom's still crying, clutching my sleeve like she's afraid to let go.

I didn't fuck it up.

I did it.

They're *proud* of me…

*****

Lunch goes by in near silence — just the soft clink of forks, the scrape of plates, the faint hum of approval breaking the quiet.

I watch every face, every flicker of expression. I listen to every small sound of contentment. This part never gets old. Feeding people — *feeding them love disguised as food* — it's a high I'll spend the rest of my life chasing.

"This is the best fucking thing I've ever eaten, Marley," Derrick says at last.

I wait for the punchline, the joke, the inevitable pun. But it never comes.

He just stares down at his empty plate, shakes his head. When he looks up, he meets my gaze and holds it. There's no flare, no sarcasm. No smirk hiding behind his eyes. Just something quieter. Something that lands deep in my chest.

"I mean it, Mars. Never. In my entire fucking life have I tasted anything better than this."

And there it is again — that damn lump in my throat.

12 | JONES

"You don't have to do that," Marley says as I start gathering plates from the table.

Simone wasn't feeling great, so Derrick took her upstairs to lie down. London and Sev went to pick up his parents from the airport, which left me here—helping, or at least pretending to while I waited for a chance to actually talk to him.

"I'm not leaving you to cook and clean up after everyone, Marley baby. This really was something else," I sing-song, stacking the last of the dishes. "I'm fucking impressed."

"Thanks, Jones." His voice is quiet but warm. "That means a hell of a lot, coming from one of the best I know."

Our eyes meet across the counter. He draws a slow breath.

"Can we talk?" he asks, searching my face.

"Yeah," I say after a beat. "That'd be good. I'll grab us some lemonades—you grab a couple of chairs by the pool?"

"Sure."

Fuck, my nerves kick up. But this conversation needs to happen.

By the time I make it out to the pool, Marley's peeled off his Henley, sitting back in nothing but a white tank.

"Damn, Marley," I say, handing him his lemonade before settling into the chair beside him. "You really did buff up. And—hell, tatted now too. You're a completely different person."

My eyes catch on the ink wrapping around his bicep. *Remi.*

"Who's Remi?" I ask before I can stop myself.

He freezes, then quickly pulls his shirt back on and shakes his head. "Another story for another time."

I let out a laugh, trying to diffuse the heaviness creeping in. "Alright, alright. I get it. The ladies are probably flocking anyway — no need to feel weird about getting one of their names inked on you. We've all been there."

"You don't have to pretend not to hate me, Jones." He shakes his head, and there's a weight in his eyes — not anger, just a kind of quiet sadness. "No one's here. I just wanted to clear the air."

Wait. What?

"What do you mean?" I ask, confusion knotting my chest.

"After I remembered what happened that night..." He exhales, leaning forward, elbows on his knees, hands covering his face like he's trying to press the memory back into silence. "I felt like shit. For using you like that. For..." He drags a hand through his hair, voice breaking on the edge of the word. "For what I did."

He turns toward me fully, eyes glassy but steady. "I should've reached out. Apologized. Explained. I was a fucking coward, and I don't blame you for hating me the way you do. I just needed to say this — to get it out — and maybe… maybe try to rebuild a friendship with you."

I'm…*dumbfounded.*

"I never—ever—hated you, Marley. I thought *you* hated me. I thought you were disgusted with me, and that's why you never reached out. Why you never came home."

How could he think that?

"Why would I have been upset with you?"

"Because I used you!"

He shoots to his feet, hands flying through the air. "I fucking *used* you as some goddamn experiment, and then conveniently forgot about it! Never called, never talked about it, just left it hanging!" His voice cracks — somewhere between anger and self-loathing. "You should despise me, Jones! *I fucking despise me!*"

I stand and reach for him, gripping his shoulder before pulling him against my chest. His whole body trembles. He's lived with the thought that I hated him this entire damn time.

God, I should've been the one to reach out. I should've fixed this years ago.

"Marley baby," I whisper, tightening my arms around him, "I could never hate you for that night. We were drunk and stupid, and I didn't do anything I didn't want to do. Not then, not ever."

My hand finds the back of his neck, holding him there until his arms finally come up around me.

"I'm sorry you've carried this alone," I say. "I'm sorry I didn't reach out and tell you sooner that we were good. Always good, Marley baby. I swear to you."

I ease him back just enough to see his face, my palms braced on his shoulders. Tears track down his cheeks.

"Do you believe me?"

He nods, a soft, broken sound escaping him before he buries himself in my arms again.

"Fuck, Marley."

"I still can't believe you told London," he says with a watery laugh, pulling back to wipe his eyes.

I let out a shaky laugh of my own. "Yeah, that wasn't intentional. Total panic moment. I haven't told anyone else. You?"

"Remi."

"Ah, the girl."

"And Mom."

Whaaaaattttt the fuck.

I do my absolute best to keep my face straight. "Oh yeah? I didn't know you told Sev. She hasn't mentioned it."

"Yeah, I told her yesterday when we went for a walk."

My head's spinning. *She knew when we… she fucking knew?*

He shakes his head, a faint smile ghosting across his lips. "Thanks for talking with me, Jones. This has really been fucking with my head."

"Is that why you haven't told the family everything?" I ask, watching him carefully.

His eyes flick toward me, wary—like he's not sure how much I actually know about *everything.*

"They'd want to be part of your victories, your life in general, Marley baby."

He looks down, shoulders drawn in, and just nods.

Before either of us can say more, the door swings open and voices flood the space. I stand, resting a hand on his shoulder.

"It's your story to tell, and your time to tell it," I say quietly. "I'm here for you, though. Not my cock—just my ears, so don't get any funny ideas."

"For fuck's sake, Jones." He groans, but it breaks into a deep, genuine laugh—the kind that shakes loose some of the weight hanging between us.

I let out a long sigh. God, that felt good. Now to find Sev and beat her with the closest blunt object — figuratively. Mostly.

When we come in, she's bent over the grocery bags, sorting and stacking like it's choreography. London is showing his parents through the house; everyone else is caught up in their own little orbits.

She looks up and the air snaps tight. My chest constricts in that familiar, ridiculous way — I've always known I love Sev, but now it's a fiercer thing, raw and loud and somehow terrifying.

I nod toward the porch, wordless. Her brow furrows the moment she catches the seriousness in my eyes, but she doesn't ask. Just slides the last bag onto the counter and follows.

She closes the door behind her gently, eyes already searching mine.
"Are you okay?" she asks, stepping closer.

She moves to sit in my lap, the way she always does when we talk like this—when it's heavy, when she wants to be near. But I stop her, hands on her shoulders, guiding her into the chair across from me.

I need my blood to rush to my brain right now. Not my cock.

She settles, slightly confused, but patient.

"Marley told you what happened between us." It wasn't a question.

She nods slowly. "He did. Yeah."

"You're not upset?"

"I was... surprised," she says carefully. "But I can't say I was upset."

She shifts, thoughtful. "Maybe a little jealous, for a second. I thought—maybe—you wanted to be with him. And honestly, I would've understood. You've always said you found him attractive, and I know you weren't lying. But Marley told me it's not like that."

She watches me now, voice gentle. "Is that what's bothering you? That I know?"

I nod, but she doesn't let the silence win. Her hand finds mine across the small table—gentle, grounding—and she keeps going.

"I understand why you didn't tell me. If it had been anyone else... I probably would've questioned it. But Marley?" She shakes her head. "That's something he wouldn't want shared without his say-so. And I respect you for respecting that."

She pauses, watching me closely now.

"I'm guessing you knew about his job already?"

I drop my gaze to my hands. Guilt tightens in my chest.

But she reaches for me again, this time cupping my jaw. Tilts my head back to her, and presses a soft kiss to my mouth.

"Chef Maverick," she murmurs, lips brushing mine. "The way he looked at you… I knew. It was something in that moment. You weren't surprised. You knew. And I'm not upset, baby."

Baby.

She's never called me that before. Not since this shift between us. Not in *this* world we're building from scratch.

And just like that—*my cock twitches*. Fucking traitor.

Her eyes catch the flicker in mine, the way my pupils dilate, and her mouth curves into a knowing smirk.

"Oh," she hums, teasing. "You liked that, didn't you?"

"Yeah," I breathe. "I did."

She leans in, the wicked glint in her eye making my blood thrum.

"Can I sit on your face later, baby?"

Jesus.

The restraint it takes not to growl, not to stand and toss her over my shoulder right here in front of God and whoever's still lurking inside the house—it's *superhuman.*

"Careful," I murmur, voice low and dark. "I'm dangerously close to making that happen right now. Porch, patio furniture, and all."

She laughs softly, but her gaze lingers—searching, serious beneath the teasing.

"Are we okay now?" she asks. "I know there's still more we all have to talk through, but I'm glad this part's off your chest. It must've been eating at you."

God. This woman.

I stand and pull her with me, wrapping my arms around her.

This is it. There will never be anyone else.

I'm *all in*. Whatever that looks like. However messy or beautiful or hard.

"The answer's yes," I say, voice rough. "But London's gotta get on one knee and ask me. That's my only condition."

I pause, smirking.

"And the ring better be the absolute *shit*."

She lets out a laugh and shakes her head. "That's going to take some convincing. But don't worry—I have my ways."

Then she leans in, eyes playful. "Can I kiss you now?"

I narrow my eyes, step back just enough to let the tease curl between us.

"Neither of you gets this mouth until I'm a married man."

Her jaw drops in mock outrage. "You wouldn't *dare*."

"Oh, Sev…" I tuck a loose strand of hair behind her ear,

letting my fingers linger. "I *fucking* dare."

<u>13</u> | JONES

Three Years Ago...

"Hi everyone — I'm the best man, and the little brother in this equation."

Marley fiddles with his hands as he stands at the mic, nerves barely hidden behind a crooked smile.

"If you know me, you already know I'm not great with words. Or timing. Or, honestly, much of anything that requires coordination or adult supervision. My brother got all of that — the patience, the drive, the steady hand. He was the one who figured things out; I was the one breaking them. Growing up, he was everything I wasn't. The straight-A student, the one who remembered to call Mom back, the one who never missed curfew. Me? I was... let's just say a work in progress."

The crowd laughs. I don't. Marley always hides behind self-deprecating humor. I've never found it funny.

"And even though I'd never admit it back then, I worshiped him. Still do, actually. He was the kind of big brother who could fix anything — my bike, my phone, my heart. And he never made me feel like I was less, even when I did. He'd just say something like,

'You'll figure it out, man. You always do.' And somehow, I believed him.

"When he met Sloane, I remember thinking, Okay, this is different. He looked lighter — like someone had found the missing piece of him the rest of us didn't even know was gone. Watching the two of you together… it's like seeing everything he taught me — loyalty, patience, love — finally reflected back at him."

He pauses, blinking fast, wiping his eyes.
Something about him is off.
Is it the wedding emotions… or the fact that he woke up in my bed this morning?

"I know I joke about being the screw-up brother, but the truth is, having him as my example is the best thing that's ever happened to me. He showed me that being a man isn't about being perfect; it's about showing up — for your people, for the hard days, for the ones you love. And he's done that every single day.

"So, to my brother — the man who taught me what solid looks like, even when I was chaos. And to Sloane — the woman who somehow makes him laugh louder and stand taller than I've ever seen. I love you both more than I can ever put into words. And if I'm ever lucky enough to be half the man he is, it'll be because of this family, and because of tonight."

He clears his throat.

I discreetly wipe at my eyes. Sev, Simone, and Derrick are openly crying. London looks stoic as ever — but the back of his neck is red. He's barely holding it together.

"So please," Marley finishes, voice thick, *"raise your glasses. To my brother, my best friend, and his beautiful wife. May your life together be loud, messy, honest, and full of the kind of love that makes everything else fade away. To the two of you — forever."*

Applause erupts, loud and uneven.

I don't know what I was expecting, but not *that*.

He steps down from the stage, accepting hugs as he moves through the crowd — but each one is brief, like he's counting the seconds until he can escape.

By the time I realize what he's doing, he's halfway out the door.

"Marley baby, where are you going in such a hurry?" I call, catching up to him.

"To the airport. Home," he says, not meeting my eyes.

"Wait, what? You're leaving now?"

"I've got stuff to take care of at home. The wedding's over."

My stomach sinks. "Mars, you can't just leave. There's still so much going on — Derrick's going to want you here."

I follow him into the elevator, then down the hall toward his room, still trying to make sense of it. His shoulders are squared, his jaw set.

"Marley…"

He stops at the door, finally looking at me. His voice cracks just slightly.

"I can't stay here, Jones. Just… leave it, okay?"

He walks into his room, letting the door shut behind him.

Is he even going to tell his family goodbye?

I wait outside of his room until he walks out, his eyes look rimshot red.

"Fuck, why are you still out here, Jones?"

"Listen, Marley."

Shit. My throat tightens.

"You're a fucking maverick, you know that? You never play it safe. You dive headfirst into *everything*—love, pain, all of it. And yeah, it wrecks you sometimes, but that's what makes you *you*. So whatever's clawing at you right now—don't let it win, okay? Hold on to your fire."

******

It's been two months since the wedding.

Two months of silence.

No one's heard from Marley.

We know he's alive — Sev reached out to his roommate through social media — but that's the only proof we've got. He hasn't called. Hasn't texted. Hasn't checked in.

Derrick and Simone were rightfully pissed that he had left the wedding so abruptly, with no word, no explanation. And I've been carrying that guilt ever since.

Because it's my fault he left.

Whatever he remembered that morning — whatever pieces of that night came back — they were enough to make him run. Even if he didn't remember *everything,* waking up naked in my bed was more than enough to spook him.

Sev's been worried sick. And I can't blame her.

******

"Did you hear that Sevynn Moore's kid started an internship at LeVeaux?"

Rocky — our delivery guy — asks it so casually as he hands me a box of eggplants that I almost drop the damn thing.

"I'm sorry, what?" The words come out sharper than I mean. I can't have heard him right.

"Yeah," he says, adjusting his cap. "He's hiding out in New Orleans, only going by Chef Maverick. Tony in logistics told me."

That can't be true. Marley's at college. He's *supposed* to be at college.
Even though I haven't seen him in months, it just doesn't ring true.

"I don't think that's right," I mutter, setting the box down harder than necessary and grabbing for the next one. "Probably just another kitchen rumor."

But when I get home, I can't shake it.
I sit down, open my laptop, and type *Chef Maverick New Orleans.*

The first article loads instantly — and there he is.

A photo of Marley, mid-pan flip, wearing a facemask and a bandana. His hair's longer now, tied back, and even with half his face covered, I'd know him anywhere.

"Culinary newcomer Chef Maverick is taking LeVeaux by storm," the article reads. *"Owner Chef Marulli praises his raw instinct and precision, saying his potential is unlike anything he's ever seen.*

Unknown to the culinary world, Chef Maverick keeps a low profile, photographed only with his mask on, stating that publicity isn't his passion — cooking is."

My chest tightens.

He hasn't told Sev.

She'd be *beaming* — hell, she'd be shouting it from the rooftops.

Why the hell is he keeping this a secret? Now I have to fucking keep it, too. I owe him that much.

******

Six Months Later

Sev's been quiet all day. It's her birthday, and even though the house is full of people and decorations, she's been waiting for one voice that never came. Marley hasn't been back to Raleigh in more than two years, and she'd hoped—really hoped—he'd show up for the surprise party. But he called London this morning to say he couldn't make it.

"Did he say why?" I'd asked.

London only shook his head. "Nope. Can't get a straight answer out of him about much of anything lately."

And that's what did me in. I keep thinking maybe if I step back, he'll come around more. Maybe if I'm not here, Sev will see her kids together again. But the truth is, I can't stop worrying. I can't stop checking. It's been months since I last looked him up, but tonight I type his name into the search bar anyway. I can't sleep after seeing Sev so damn sad all day, on her day.

The results load, one after another, and my chest tightens as I scroll.

Chef Maverick — Executive Chef.

Chef Maverick — Rising Star of the Year.

Article after article, hardly any pictures, but his name is attached to every kind of praise you could imagine. He's thriving. Building something real. And no one here knows a thing about it.

He's kept it to himself, just like he's kept all of us at arm's length. I should tell Sev—she'd be over the moon, bragging to anyone who would listen—but it's not my story to tell. He earned this on his own, away from all of us.

I lean back in my chair and stare at the photo on the screen. His hair's longer now, his shoulders broader, his eyes—God, his eyes—focused in a way I've never seen before.

"I'm proud of you, Marley baby," I whisper. The words feel heavy and right, and I hope, wherever he is, he hears them.

"I'll take the blackened mahi-mahi with citrus slaw and sweet potato mash," I tell the server, handing him our menus with a polite smile.

Simone, Derrick, and I slipped out for dinner while London and Mom got his parents settled in. Tomorrow, London's siblings get back after taking off for a couple of days, and the festivities officially begin.

"You really are on a health kick," Derrick says, grinning. "Old Mars would've gone for the cheesiest, meatiest thing on the menu."

I laugh, even though it's half-hearted. I'm hoping my nerves calm down enough tonight to tell them what's actually been going on in my life — more than the job, more than what they think they know. But today's already been heavy enough.

"Yeah," I say, swirling the condensation on my water glass. "I don't even really miss the other stuff. I've got cheat days here and there, but it's kind of second nature now."

I take a slow sip of my water, pretending to study the condensation on the glass. "So. Babies, am I right?"

Simone's eyes go wide. Derrick's mouth falls open.

"What… uh…" Derrick stammers, glancing at Simone. "What *about* babies?" His voice hits a pitch I didn't know he had.

"I don't know." I shrug, trying to sound casual and failing spectacularly. "I was just thinking about babies. You know, their tiny little toes and smushy faces." I make a motion like I'm squishing invisible baby cheeks between my fingers. "How do you two feel about… babies?"

"Neutral," Simone says quickly, taking a giant gulp of her lemonade. "We are *defo* neutral on the subject." She punctuates it with a pop of her lips.

"Defo. Definitely. Good word choice, baby. Neutral. Yes." Derrick nods too fast, eyes darting anywhere but mine.

I narrow my eyes at them both. "Guys."

They both freeze.

"Guys." I lean forward, lowering my voice. "I *know*."

"What do you know?" Derrick *yells*.

"Ricky, you're yelling," Simone stage-whispers, eyes wide.

"I'm yelling. You're right." He nods, pats her hand once like they're in crisis counseling, then turns back to me — same exact pitch, same exact volume. "What do you *know*?!"

Simone groans, dragging a hand down her face. "That I'm pregnant, you *idiot*."

"*WHAT?!*" Derrick screeches, whipping his head toward

Simone so fast his chair nearly topples. A couple of nearby tables turn to look.

I lose it — laughing so hard my stomach aches. This fucking guy.

"Pregnant?!" he repeats, eyes wide, voice climbing an octave higher.

"Lower your voice, Ricky," Simone hisses, trying to smile through her embarrassment.

"And how does *Marley* know before *me?!*" he screeches again, somehow even louder. "This is not funny, Marley."

"It really is," I say, trying not to grin. "I thought you knew."

"How *did* you know?" Simone asks, crossing her arms.

Derrick is still staring at the side of her head, wide-eyed, waiting for her to acknowledge him.

"You were pretending to drink," I explain, taking a sip of water like this is a perfectly normal conversation. "I saw you dump a couple of shots. Also, I might've… purposefully made you puke. Twice."

She frowns. "You *what?*"

"Research," I say with a shrug. "I needed to be sure."

"Uh, *helloooo?*" Derrick taps her shoulder, leaning in so close his nose almost brushes her cheek.

Simone closes her eyes, takes a steadying breath, then turns to him. She cups his face in her hands and kisses him softly.

"Ricky," she murmurs, "I'm pregnant."

"Well, I got *that* part!" he yells, throwing his hands up.

"When I asked you about how you felt about having a baby," she says, fighting a smile, "you had a *panic attack*. So I haven't exactly had the courage to bring it up again."

"You're not very observant, bro," I tease, leaning back in my chair. "You live with the woman, and I figured it out in less than a day."

Simone laughs, shaking her head. "You are *so* not helping, Marley." She glances at Derrick, still grinning. "But… he's not wrong. I've had morning sickness for three weeks straight now."

Derrick blinks, stunned. "I thought you had a stomach bug!"

"Well, here we are." Simone takes his hands in hers, her smile soft. "Are you okay, baby?"

God, I love these two. I've missed them.

Derrick exhales and leans in to kiss her, finally settling his nerves. "I can't believe he figured it out before me," he pouts, then grins through it. "But I'm okay. I just hope it's a girl—and that she looks like you."

Tears gather in both their eyes.

"When are you announcing?" I ask once their moment breaks into soft laughter.

"Anytime now that this *lughead* knows," Simone says, elbowing him in the side.

"Guess I'm the hot one *and* the smart one, now," I add with a wide grin.

Derrick gasps dramatically, pressing a hand to his chest.

"Oh my God, do *not* get him started," Simone warns,

shaking her head.

"I am *so* the hot one, motherfucker," Derrick snarls, voice rising with mock outrage.

"Sure, buddy," I chuckle, taking another sip of my water.

Before he can fire back—and he's *definitely* about to, judging by the red creeping up his neck—the waiter appears with our food.

"Perfect timing, my man," I say, leaning back and giving Derrick a wink.

"I'm not trying to fucking hide you, Remi. That's not what this is about, and you know it. It's just not the right time. I'm sorry."

I freeze mid-step, coffee in hand, the steam curling up between my fingers. Marley's voice is sharper than usual — raw and splintered at the edges. It slices through the quiet of the hallway, stopping me cold.

I should keep walking. I know I should. But something in his tone roots me there.

"Yes, I talked to Jones." A pause. The sound of his breath, uneven.

Are they arguing about me?

"No! Of course, nothing fucking happened between us. Where is this coming from, Remi? You've done a complete 180 since the last time we talked! "

Another beat of silence. Then a sigh—long, tired, the kind

that sounds like surrender. The bed creaks; I can picture him sitting down, rubbing a hand over his face.

"I don't want to fight with you," he says, softer now. "I'm sorry I upset you. I love you."

I start to back away quietly, hoping my retreat won't betray me. But apparently the universe has a personal vendetta, because my heel catches the edge of the hallway rug and I stumble hard. My shoulder slams into the wall, one of the cups slips from my grip, and it hits the floor—shattering.

The sound is sharp enough to slice through the air, and within seconds, Marley's door swings open.

He's standing there, wide-eyed and breathless, panic written all over his face. Probably wondering how much I heard.

"I'll call you back," he says abruptly, sliding his phone into his back pocket. His voice is calm, but the tension in his jaw gives him away.

"Are you okay?" he asks, already moving—grabbing a towel from his chair and crouching to blot the mess before I can even answer.

"I'm fine." My voice comes out thinner than I mean it to. I avoid his eyes like a coward and reach for the scattered shards of glass instead. "I was bringing you a cup of coffee, but didn't want to interrupt. Apparently, the rug had other plans."

"You can just admit that you fell for me, Jones," he says without missing a beat. "I won't tell anyone."

Oh, don't you fucking dare, Marley Moore. For fuck's sake.

I let out a laugh—short, incredulous, mostly to keep from throwing the remaining coffee at his smug face. "Oh, how the tables have turned."

His grin flickers, softer than usual, and for one dizzying second, I can't tell if we're joking anymore.

"So…" I say, as we both stand. Him holding a coffee-stained towel, me clutching a handful of glass like an idiot. "Remi… she's your girlfriend?"

I nod toward the tattoo on his arm, the one he always covers but never quite hides.

He drags a hand through his hair, the gesture as much exhaustion as habit. "It's complicated."

"Isn't it always."

He lets out a low chuckle. "Yeah."

"Wanna talk about it?"

"I…" He hesitates, thumb rubbing the back of his neck. "I do. But, uh—"

Before he can finish, Sev's voice cuts through the house. "Marley! Derrick! Your father's here!"

Every muscle in his body tenses. His shoulders slump; the life drains right out of his face.

"Fuck," he mutters. "I thought he wasn't coming. *Fuck.*"

"Hey…" I reach out, resting a hand on his shoulder. The contact is small but steady. "We'll keep him in line. Don't worry about him."

"It's not—" He exhales, the fight leaving him mid-sentence. "Ugh. Thanks, Jones."

He squeezes my hand once before stepping back. "Tell Mom I'll be down in five, would you?"

I walk downstairs and toss the glass into the trash, already dreading the sight of that bastard's face. I swear, I feel *violent* urges around him.

Jaxon and Sev have managed to get... cordial over the past couple of years. He lives about an hour outside of town now with his wife, Jessica, and their two-year-old daughter, Lilian. Sev tries to keep the peace — for the kids' sake. Lilian is Marley and Derrick's little sister, after all.

She's a sweet kid. She clings to me every time I walk in the room, which drives Jaxon absolutely insane. Honestly, it's the only redeeming part of him showing up. Lilian is tiny for her age, all big blonde curls and ocean-blue eyes — a doll that makes me wonder, stupidly and suddenly, what it would be like to have kids of my own someday.

"Joey!" Lilian squeals the second she sees me, wiggling out of Jaxon's arms as I round the corner.

"Hey, Lili Bug!" I grin, crouching just in time to catch her as she runs into me. "How's my girl?"

She giggles — that deep-belly kind that makes the world feel less sharp for a second. She loves it when I call her *my girl*. I hoist her onto my hip and head toward the others, then glance over at Jaxon.

"Jax," I say, stretching out my hand with a smug smile. "Good to see you."

His handshake is as fake as his charm — firm enough to prove a point, but not enough to feel human.

"Hey, Jennifer," I add, not even glancing her way.

"Jessica," she corrects softly, after a deep, steadying breath.

"Right. So sorry about that."

I'm such an asshole.

"Jones…" Sev warns, her tone sharp enough to cut glass.

I lift my free hand in surrender. "Fine. *Sorry, Jessica.* How are you?"

She opens her mouth to answer, but I barrel right over her. "Good, glad to hear it."

Then I pivot, turning my back and walking with Lilian toward the kitchen. "You want something to drink, Lili-Bug?"

Her little head nods against my shoulder, blissfully unaware of the tension buzzing behind us. I hold her close as I grab a juice box from the fridge, then set her gently on the counter. She's so fucking cute it hurts.

I've never really wanted kids. I love the *idea* of them — the laughter, the tiny hands, the chaos — but not for myself. I'm happy being the cool uncle. *Uncle Joey* for now, maybe *Uncle Jones* when she can finally pronounce it. Either way, I'll take it. It fits.

She sips her juice and hums quietly, focused on her latest mission: braiding my hair with sticky little fingers. I let her, half-listening to the conversation happening across the room.

If you squinted, you'd think they all looked normal — two couples, a family gathering, polite smiles and soft laughter. But I know better. I know how Jaxon humiliated Sev, over and over, until she stopped trying to fight back. And Jessica — sweet, perfect Jessica — slid right in and helped him finish the job. She broke a home. She broke *my* Sev.

So yeah, I get why Sev keeps the peace — for the kids, for appearances — but every time I see them standing here pretending, I can feel my teeth grind.

Jaxon stands as soon as Marley and Derrick walk in. "Hey, Dad," they say in unison, crossing the room and extending their hands.

It's the same dance every time. He expects hugs; they offer handshakes. His face falls, and I can almost hear the echo of disappointment bouncing off the walls. Their relationship exists purely out of obligation now. Nothing more.

"Hey, boys. How are things?" Jaxon asks, forcing a smile.

I flinch as Lilian yanks too hard on a knotted section of my braid. "Easy, Bug," I whisper, forcing a laugh, but my eyes never leave the man across the room.

Marley looks like he's about to snap. His hands fidget; his eyes jump from face to face like someone trying to find a door. Whatever's building under his skin is close to boiling over.

I lean forward on the counter, angling to catch fragments of the conversation. Derrick's talking, but I can't make out the words. Lilian has better ideas: she tugs my head back again, grinning like she's winning a game.

And that's why I can't have kids of my own. Because in that exact second, I'm seriously tempted to yank her braid back in petty, glorious retaliation — which, last I checked, is frowned upon and also probably a one-way ticket to Uncle *Joey* being banned from birthday parties for life.

I half-listen as Derrick and Dad drone on about Dad's latest sports car — because, of course, sports cars are *their* thing. Always have been.

I can tell Derrick's trying to patch things up, ease the tension, maybe bring their relationship back to something that resembles normal. If not for himself, then for Lilian's sake.

I haven't been as willing.

And maybe that makes me selfish. But I don't care. I want nothing to do with him or Jessica. They blew up our family and walked away like it was some damn experiment gone wrong.

I still love Dad. But the thing is, I hate him just as fucking much.

"Did you hear me, Mars?"

My head lifts like it's underwater. I blink, caught halfway between memory and this too-bright room.

"Sorry," I say, clearing my throat. "What were you

asking?"

Dad's smile doesn't falter, like he's used to me checking out. "You've filled out," he says, nodding toward my shoulders. "Buffed up pretty good. What's your gym routine look like these days?"

Really? That's the opening line?

I sit back, resting the glass against my lips, letting the words find their edge before I speak. "Nothing complicated. I get up early. Hit the gym hard. Pretend the past doesn't exist. Then I do it all again the next day."

Silence hums. I let it sit there like a truth no one asked for.

He laughs with an incredulous chuckle, like he thinks I'm joking.

I'm not.

Mom must feel it too—whatever just cracked beneath the surface—because she reaches across and places a hand on my knee. "Marley's been working as an Executive Chef at LeVeaux," she says gently, like it's a gift she's offering him.

Dad's brows rise, genuinely surprised. "No shit? That's incredible."

Jessica smiles a little too wide. "That's really great to hear, Mars."

"It's Marley," I correct, without looking at her. My voice stays even, but the tone does the work.

She lowers her gaze, her smile faltering. "Sorry. Marley. That's really great. Congratulations."

And just like that, I'm the asshole again.

Dad leans forward a little, like he's trying to close a gap I'm not ready to bridge. "How long have you been there? Seriously, that's something to be proud of."

I shift in my seat, shrugging. "A year and a half as Executive Chef. And I didn't do it for your pride."

The words hang there longer than I meant them to. Heavy. Sharper than I'd intended.

I close my eyes for a second. "Sorry," I add, softer. "Didn't mean that to come out like it did."

Across the room, I can feel the temperature shift. Everyone's looking at me like I'm made of flint and they're just waiting for the spark.

But Dad doesn't flinch. He just nods, something soft pulling at the corner of his mouth.
"It's okay, son. I know things... they didn't get tied up the right way. I own my part in that. I'm not asking for anything here. Just—" he pauses, clears his throat, the words catching, "—it's just good to see you."

His voice is steady, but his eyes—glassy, shining in that way that makes you feel twelve years old and furious again—shift to London as he pivots to safer ground. Something about the design process. Something easier to talk about than *me*.

I glance at Mom. She's already watching. That sad little smile on her face—the kind that says she's proud but also sorry. Always sorry. Always somewhere between apology and prayer.

I can't sit in this room a second longer.

"I'm gonna step out for a bit," I say quietly to no one in particular.

They all just nod like they were waiting for me to crack first. Like they had bets on how long I'd last.

Jones watches me as I pass. Doesn't say a word, just gives me a small nod—the kind men give each other when they know a storm's coming and it's not their place to try and stop it.

Outside, I shut the door behind me and exhale so hard it feels like my lungs collapse. The quiet hits like a slap.

I can't shake this edge.

I lean against the porch railing and close my eyes. The shame's back. That old, thick kind—the kind that clings like oil and never really scrubs off. I need to tell them. About Remi. About the house. About all of it. But the second I start, I see their faces when I told them about LeVeaux.

Fucking dishes.

They thought I was a damn dishwasher. Like that was the height of what I could achieve. Like that's all I'd ever be. Even if it were, they should just be fucking proud. And that's what stings—the job's not the shame. The way they looked at me is.

They think so fucking little of me. And even though I've done everything to prove them wrong, somehow, I still feel like the screw-up. The dropout. The disappointment. Like no matter how far I climb, I'll always be that kid who left Raleigh in shame and never really came back.

And maybe they don't even see me that way anymore. Maybe it's just me. Still carrying the version of myself they gave up on.

I press my palms into my eyes until stars burst behind them. Remi should be here. I should've told everyone by now.

About us. About why I can't sleep at night when we fight the way we did this morning.

But I didn't.

And now the wedding games start tonight, and I'm alone. Because I was too much of a fucking coward to tell the truth. Too scared to own what I want. Too late to fix what I broke.

And it's all starting to unravel—every thread I've tried to hold in place for the sake of appearances, for the sake of peace.

I'm unraveling.

The door opens behind me with the softest click, and I don't need to turn around to know it's Mom. I can feel the worry in the air.

"I'm fine, Mom. Promise." I say, staring out across the yard. "Just needed some air."

But my breath catches.
Because it's not my mother.
It's *Jessica*.

She steps beside me without a word, eyes fixed straight ahead toward the pool house like we're just two people admiring the scenery. But her voice doesn't match the view.

"I've never gotten the chance to apologize to you, Marley," she says softly, "not really."

I don't answer. I don't trust my mouth to move without the rest of me falling apart.

"I know you all hate me. And I get it. I do. When Jaxon and I first started seeing each other, he told me that he and your mom were already separated. I didn't question it. I wanted to believe him." She pauses, like the next part physically hurts.

"But I found out that wasn't entirely true. And I stayed anyway. I stayed because I was already in love with him. That doesn't excuse what I did. Nothing does or ever will."

Her eyes are wet. But she doesn't blink them away. She lets the tears fall.

I keep my grip on the railing, jaw tight. I don't know what she wants from me. Redemption? Permission to forgive herself? I can't give her either of those things.

"I didn't want to come here for the wedding," she adds, voice nearly a whisper now. "I told Jaxon I wouldn't. But your mom called me. She asked me to be here. Said maybe it was time. That we'd all been holding onto pain for too long."

That punches a hole right through my chest.

"What?" I finally look at her, startled.

She nods, still watching the yard. "She reached out to me. She said she didn't want this weekend to carry the same weight the last few years have. She asked me to come for the sake of...moving forward, I guess."

She finally turns to me then.

"I know it's not my place to be, but I want you to know that I *am* proud of you, Marley. I see how hard you've worked to become someone you're proud of. And I know what it feels like... to try and outrun the version of yourself people still think you are. It's exhausting. But I see you."

There's no pity in her voice. No performance. And before I can find anything to say—anything that doesn't sound like a wound—she nods once and turns to walk away.

"Jessica?" I say, keeping my back to her, eyes locked on the horizon.

She pauses. "Yeah?"

"You can call me Mars."

That's all I've got. The best I can offer right now. But the soft hitch in her breath… the quiet sob she doesn't try to hide…

It tells me it's enough.

"Thanks… Mars."

The door clicks shut behind her, and I'm alone again.

Well. Fuck.

"GO GO GO!" Dad shouts as we hop our way down the racing path, burlap sacks flapping around our legs. "They're closing in!"

We'd been paired up for the doubles sack race — and for the sake of crushing Mom and Derrick's winning streak, I'll allow it. They always win. Every damn year. And then we have to suffer through their smug, trophy-swinging victory laps until the next games.

But not this time. Me and Dad are hauling ass.

"Jesus Christ, my lungs are about to collapse," Dad pants as we round the last obstacle and head for the finish line.

"Don't you fucking punk out on me, old man," I wheeze. "We cannot let them win."

"Damn it, Mother, where is your stamina?!" Derrick shouts from behind us.

I'm dying, but I can't laugh—I'll fall.

"You're not hopping when I hop!" Mom fires back, pure exasperation.

Me and Dad cross the finish line with one final launch, hopping around like teenage boys instead of two grown-ass men. Derrick drops to his knees, fists raised to the sky like he's in a telenovela. "Noooooooo!"

Mom giggles and shoves my arm. "You cheated!"

"How can one cheat at sack races, Mother?" I ask, grinning like a smug bastard. "Please, enlighten me." This is the vendication I needed after the massacre at that damn air hockey table.

Before she can answer, London and his sister Sloane limp across the finish line in third, collapsing into the grass with matching groans.

"These are not the same sacks," London huffs. "Why are they so heavy?"

"Maybe you're not the same young chicken you once were, Lon," I tease, knowing exactly what I'm doing.

He blinks. "Oh, hell no."

London springs up and charges me like a linebacker, shoulder first, and we're instantly sparring. It's playful—he's not trying to hurt me, just overpower me. But he can't. In one clean move, I sweep his legs and pin him to the ground with a wrestling hold.

"Goddammit," he mutters, tapping out.

"You been taking judo now, too?" he pants. "Holy fucking hell."

I chuckle and take his hand, helping him up. "Krav Maga."

London gives me a once-over, eyes narrowing. "You're annoying."

I just laugh.

Then London pulls me into a hug, clapping my back hard. "Proud of you, my boy."

I glance over his shoulder and catch Dad watching us. His smile's tight, but his eyes are soft—and maybe a little sad. I haven't hugged him in years. And seeing me like this—open, laughing, being embraced by someone else—yeah, I can imagine how that lands.

"Krav Maga?" Sloane asks, brushing grass off her arms. She and London took a few good tumbles. "That's so hot."

"No!" Derrick shouts, already halfway to a breakdown. "It's not hot! It's—it's normal! It's a totally normal thing to do! Marley's not hot, he's NORMAL!"

Everyone freezes.

Then Sloane tilts her head, totally unbothered. "Uh-huh. You scream that a lot for someone who's not jealous of your hot brother."

"Jealous?!" Derrick's voice jumps an octave. He points at me like I just confessed to being the Antichrist. "He eats grilled chicken and protein powder gravy! He does burpees… for fun! This isn't jealousy, Sloane—it's concern!"

I break—bent at the waist, howling. Even Sloane snorts.

"Let's ease up on calling my boy hot, little sis," London cuts in, scrubbing a hand down his face like he needs bleach for his brain. "Thanks—I just ate."

"He's not your boy," Dad says sharply.

Wait a fucking minute now.

London's jaw ticks, but he doesn't bite. Doesn't even blink at the bait, even though the tension slices through the air like a cleaver.

"Yet being the operative word, Jax," London replies smoothly, lips quirking into a smug, unbothered grin.

And I swear, if Dad starts shit at this wedding, I will burn this whole picturesque weekend to the ground. He catches my glare—sees my fists clenched, my body wound like a spring— and backs down.

"Sorry," he mutters, tone gruff. "That was a dick thing to say. I didn't mean any offense by it."

"None taken," London says, casually slinging an arm across my shoulder and stepping into my line of sight, a wall between me and the man who made me. His voice stays calm, light. "It's all good, Mars. Let's go get cleaned up for the welcome dinner. You're sweaty as hell, and now I've gotta stand next to you in pictures."

I nod, jaw tight—but grateful.

It might seem strange that London and I are this close, considering I haven't really been home since their wedding. But he's made it a point to keep Derrick and me in his orbit. He texts every day. Calls when he can. I've asked him for advice about stocks, cars, hell—even how to negotiate a raise.

He doesn't know the full scope of what's going on in my life, and I carry that guilt like extra weight in my bones. But if anyone's earned the title of father figure these last few years…it's him.

He knows my temper. Knows the cracks in my armor I

don't show most people. He's one of the only ones who knows what happened with Jones.

And he saw it—how close I was to losing it when Dad made that snide-ass comment. He stepped in. De-escalated. Protected me from myself without making a scene.

I respect the hell out of him. Not just for what he does, but for how he does it. For the way he treats Mom like she's the center of his world. For being the kind of man who shows up, not for show, but because that's just who he is.

A real family man.

The kind I never thought I'd want to be.

I glance over and catch Mom riding on Jones' back, her arms slung around his neck as they both giggle like kids. It's playful. Easy. Familiar.

"It doesn't bother you—how close they are?" I ask London as we walk toward the house. My voice stays low, respectful.

London looks over at them and smiles—no trace of insecurity, not even in the corners of his mouth.

"Not at all." He stops walking, like he's weighing whether to say more. "Happiness doesn't always look the same for everyone. You define it. You live with it. Your mom's happiness is all that matters to me… no matter what that looks like. Understand?"

I feel like he's saying more than just those words—but I nod anyway. Maybe Mom finally talked to him. I just want her to be happy, too. All of them. No matter what that looks like.

"Yeah. I hear you."

"Good man," he says, and ruffles my hair like I'm twelve.

"You smell like you escaped a barn."

"Ha ha!" Derrick cackles, pointing like a damn toddler. "You smell!"

Before he can pass, London sticks out a foot, and Derrick crashes to the ground with all the grace of a cartoon character.

"Traitor!" he shouts, scrambling up as London reaches to help. "Don't you touch me, Brutus!"

"Oh, Ricky…" London smirks.

"That's Mr. Moore to you. Good day!"

"God, he's such a drama queen," Simone mutters, trailing behind, one hand resting protectively on her stomach.

London notices. "You okay, honey?" he asks, eyes flicking to where her fingers hover.

Her eyes dart to me—brief, but loud—and back to London. "Yeah. Just... yeah."

"Still feeling those eggs?" I offer casually, matching her glance with one of my own. "They messed me up, too. Been feeling it since that night."

She exhales, tension riding the breath. "Right? Ugh, yeah." Her eyes won't settle. "I better go get dressed."

And she's gone, quick as a whisper.

London watches the door close behind her. "She seem okay to you?"

I keep my face neutral, give a slow shrug. "Yeah. They were really bad eggs."

We both know that's a bullshit excuse.

Only difference is—he's guessing. I'm not.

Yet another damn secret....

"Did you enjoy the games and the welcome dinner, Sevynn?" London murmurs against Sev's neck, his voice low and smooth as aged whiskey. One hand is wrapped firmly around her throat, the other pressed flat against her stomach, holding her tight to him.

Her head tilts back against his shoulder with a breathy moan as his teeth graze the column of her throat.

She nods, lips parted, but he isn't having that.

"Use your words, baby."

"Yes," she gasps. "I enjoyed today. So much."

His mouth curves into a smile against her skin, lips brushing the delicate flutter of her pulse—*pleased*.

But his eyes? They're on *me*.

"Good girl," London murmurs, his voice thick with heat and authority.

Dinner ended hours ago. The house is quiet, dimly lit, and utterly still. Everyone has slipped off to their rooms and cabins, out of sight and out of mind. But here, in this charged pocket of silence—Sev has been anything but subtle.

She started with London. Teasing touches. Lingering looks. But her eyes stayed on me, too. Every time her fingers wandered under his shirt, every time she kissed the corner of his mouth instead of the center… she was staring at me like she was daring me to move. Daring me to renege on my word, that they couldn't have me until we were bound.

Now I'm seated in the corner chair—London's command—my hands gripping the armrests because they're the only thing tethering me to sanity. That's all I'm allowed to do. Watch. Obey.

Sev shifts in London's hold, her back arching as his hand trails up her body, slow and possessive. She moans again, a sound designed to unravel me.

And it's *working*.

London glances over his shoulder, a wicked glint in his eye.

"You still good, Jones?"

Not Edward. *Jones.*

The bastard.

My jaw tightens, knuckles turning white against the chair. "You know I am."

Sev's lips curl into a smile—slow, knowing, just shy of wicked. She's in control. Even when she pretends not to be. *Especially* when she pretends not to be.

"Then don't move," he says. He drags his mouth along the

line of her jaw, savoring her like something rare. Dangerous.
"You don't want to partake until we're married?"
His eyes flick to mine—amused and smug. "Then you sit there... and you *watch*."

I'm rethinking *all* of my life choices as I shift in my seat, adjusting myself in my pants. Nothing's helping. Not the chair. Not the rule I set. Not the steel grip I'm trying to keep on my composure.

London lifts Sev's dress over her head, unrushed and purposeful, and lets it slip to the floor.

She's left standing in nothing but black thigh-high stockings and a black lace thong—her skin golden in the soft lamplight, curves full and unapologetic.

She's put on weight over the last few years—fifteen pounds, maybe more—and every single ounce has declared *war* on my self-control. Her hips. Her thighs. The softness at her waist. The weight in her breasts. It's all fucking *devastating*.

She's the most beautiful thing I've ever seen.

My fingers dig into my thighs, hard.

Her eyes cut to mine, as she leans back into London's chest like a throne she was born to rule from.

"Is our girl teasing you, Jones?" London asks, his tone threaded with playfulness and hunger in equal measure. The way he speaks when he already knows the answer, but wants to make me say it anyway.

His hand drifts up her stomach, palm flat and steady as he maps her body like familiar terrain. When he cups her breast, his thumb brushes across her nipple with practiced ease, and Sev lets out a gasp, as her body arches into the touch. Her lips part, lashes fluttering, and I swear to God I can feel the sound she makes like it's crawling down my spine.

I grit my teeth, trying not to shift in my seat, but it's useless. The chair creaks under me like it's bearing witness.

"She's doing more than teasing," I manage.

London hums at that, gaze never leaving mine as he lowers his mouth to the curve of her shoulder and bites—just enough to make her flinch and shiver, she lets out a soft moan. He kisses the same spot, soothing the sting with his tongue, and then moves.

He guides her to the bed, not with force, but with that quiet authority he wears like a second skin. He walks her forward until she stands just a few feet in front of me, close enough to feel like a threat, far enough that I can't reach.

He sits first, spreading his legs and settling back like he owns the world, then pulls her gently into his lap. Sev settles between his thighs, her back to his chest.

"Legs open, baby," he whispers.

Sev parts her thighs without hesitation. The black lace thong barely covers anything, and the way it clings to the wet heat between her legs makes it even worse. My eyes drag over her. he's everything. Every curve. Every breath. Every drop of power she pretends not to hold.

I'm salivating. I'm fucking *ruined*.

London's hand slides down again, and he slips his fingers beneath the fabric, pulling it aside like he's unwrapping a gift he already knows by heart.

And then he looks at me. "Tell me, Jones," he says, with that wicked glint in his eyes sharpening. "Is our girl soaked yet?"

I swallow hard, the movement nearly painful, like my throat's closing in around the truth.

She is. *God, she is.*

I can see it—glistening where London's fingers have pulled the lace aside, the slick shine of her arousal catching the soft lamplight. I can *smell* it, too. That warm, dizzying mix of her scent and his skin and the lingering ghost of what we did the last time I was allowed to touch her.

I want to answer without words. I want to fall to my knees and taste her instead. But I don't.

I keep my grip on the chair, fingers dug into the armrests like claws, legs wide for balance, because I know if I shift even slightly, I'm going to do something *reckless*. And if they are serious about this, I need to hold my ground.

So, I lift my gaze from her thighs. He's watching me with a calm sort of cruelty. Testing the edge of my control.

"Yes," I say, strained. "She's soaked."

Sev's breath catches. London hums his approval, fingers stroking her gently now—taunting, not quite giving her what she wants.

"Good," he says, and leans in to kiss her neck, soft and slow, before turning his gaze back to me. "Because she's going to stay that way for a while."

His fingers moved deliberately between her thighs, circling with devastating patience. He dipped inside her, just once, and repeated the motion. Over and over. Each stroke measured, dragging her higher but never letting her fall.

She whimpered, low and breathless, hips shifting restlessly in his lap. But he kept her steady. One arm coiled tightly around her waist, the other working her in that slow, consuming rhythm that made her shudder and gasp.

And the whole time—his eyes never left me.

"I'm going to tell you a story, Jones." His voice was even, almost gentle.

"Eyes on me."

I hadn't realized I'd dropped my gaze until he said it. My mouth was slightly open, my eyes glued to the place where his hand disappeared between her thighs—the stretch of his wrist, the veins rippling like a map across his forearm, the tension in his muscles as he worked her.

It was mesmerizing. And it was killing me.

I forced my gaze back to his. "Okay," I breathed. It was the only word I could manage.

He nodded, just once. Then he spoke.

"When I was in my first year of college, I had a relationship with a man. His name was Baxley."

There was no hesitation. No fear in the words. But there was a weight. A history.

Sev moaned, her hips chasing his hand now, her head tilted back against his shoulder. Her breath hitched every time he brushed that spot inside her, her legs trembling, thighs quivering. But still, she didn't speak.

London pressed a kiss to the side of her throat, then looked back at me, his eyes darker now.

"I hid him from everyone. My closest friends. My family. It

wasn't something guys like me were supposed to do."

He didn't need to elaborate. I heard it in his voice. *Southern roots. Catholic guilt. A lifetime of expectations pressed into his skin like fingerprints left too long.*

His fingers slowed again—torturous, teasing. Sev whimpered, a soft cry of protest escaping her lips, but London only smiled. His hold on her tightened, pulling her back against his chest.

"When I refused to come out for him," he continued quietly, "when I wouldn't claim him publicly... he left me. We'd been together two years in secret, and I loved him deeply."

I didn't know if she'd heard this story before. If she knew the name, or the pain behind it. She didn't speak. Didn't open her eyes. But her body arched, mouth parting around a silent gasp, her hips still rocking in his lap.

And I... *God,* I sat there like I was nailed to the chair. Watching. Listening. Burning.

London's movements had turned relentless now. In. Out. Circle. The rhythm was merciless, precise. Sev's back was arched so high she looked like a bow strung too tight, like she might snap from the tension at any moment.

"Almost, baby," he murmured against her neck. "Almost. I'll let you come soon."

He kissed the curve of her throat with aching tenderness, like his lips could soothe the storm building in her body. Then his eyes found mine again.

And I swear to God—I forgot how to breathe.

I was mesmerized.

Not just by what he was doing to her.

But by *him*.

By this impossible, infuriating, devastating man with *so much control* in his hands and something even deeper buried in his eyes.

"I closed the door on that part of my life a long time ago," he said softly, voice low and frayed at the edges, like he was stitching it together as he spoke. "But you… you knocked it down with a sledgehammer, Jones."

His fingers never stopped moving. Neither did hers—her hands were wrapped around the back of his neck, arms stretched above her head, clutching him like he was the only thing keeping her tethered to the earth.

"I haven't wanted a man like I want you. Not ever."

His voice cracked, just slightly. Just enough to carve into me.

"I love you," he said. "I love you more than I've ever admitted out loud."

My chest shattered. Just *split*, right down the center.

Sev's breaths had turned chaotic. She was gasping now, right on the edge. Her body trembling in his lap like she was trying to hold back, but couldn't.

London shifted, held her tighter, and brought his lips to her ear.

"I'll get on one knee," he said with a tone of promise. "When I have the ring you deserve." His eyes never left mine. "But I can't picture our lives without you in it. I can't picture our bed—our future—without *you*."

Then he said it. No hesitation. No second-guessing. "So I'm

asking. For the first time. *Marry us*, Edward."

He paused. Just long enough to let the world stop spinning.

"Marry us... and come claim our girl—" His voice dropped to a growl, deep and dark. "—as she comes in your mouth."

Before I could respond—before I could *breathe*—Sev started to shatter.

"*Please*. Fuck. *Oh God*. Pleeeeeaaaasssseeeee—"

The word broke apart on a scream as London kept her orgasm teetering at the edge, her body locking tight with it, every muscle pulled like a bowstring.

"Yes. *Fuck*." I was already moving, dropping to my knees between her thighs like gravity had snapped its fingers.

My eyes stayed on London's the whole time.

His eyes were glassy now. Full. Wrecked.

"Come, baby," London growled, voice pitched low in her ear, just before he thrust three fingers inside her.

She broke.

Her whole body jolted, a sharp cry catching in her throat as she *gushed* over his hand, hips snapping forward, thighs shaking. My hands slid under her legs, spreading her open wider as I leaned in and covered her with my mouth.

She was soaked. Still pulsing. Still coming.

And I devoured her.

My mouth didn't leave her for a second—locked over her, tongue stroking deep, slow, purposeful, coaxing out every last tremor. Every flick dragged more from her, and I took it greedily, like I needed her to live. My hands gripped her thighs, holding her open for me, fingers digging into soft, trembling flesh I never wanted to let go of.

"There she is," London murmured above us, his voice deep with pride. One of his hands slid over her chest, kneading her breast, thumb brushing across her nipple until she whimpered. "My good girl. So fucking beautiful when you break."

Her body arched between us, pliant and strung tight.

And just like that—*another wave* started building.

She was still coming down, and already, I could feel it— her body winding up again beneath my mouth, her hips starting to rock, her gasps sharpening.

I'd been with women before. I'd gone down on women before. But this wasn't sex. This was something else. Something I was *inside of*, with no way back out.

"You gonna come again on Edward's tongue, baby?" London asked, fingers still teasing her breast as he leaned in to bite her earlobe, slow and soft.

"Yes," she cried out. "Yes—fuck—Jones! *Oh God!*"

Her whole body convulsed, and I felt it. *Felt her* break open around my mouth again, soaking me, thighs clamping hard around my head.

And that was all it took.

London's hand slipped to the back of my head, his fingers threading through my hair, dragging his nails along the base of my skull.

It was too much.
All of it.

The taste of her. Her voice screaming my name. His praise

in my ear. His hand in my hair.

I came.

Hard.

In my pants. No one touching me. No warning. Just the sudden, uncontrollable rush that overtook every inch of me like a wave I couldn't escape. I moaned into her, face buried between her thighs, eyes screwed shut as I rode it out, shuddering.

"Good fucking boy," London growled, his voice dark and steady above the rush still pulsing in my body. "I can't wait to make you mine, Edward."

"Fuck." I breathed out, dropping my head to Sev's thigh, panting.

There was no going back.
Not after this.
Not ever. I am theirs. I just hope my heart can take it.

Today was a good day.

I've decided I'm going to tell them everything tomorrow. It's been long enough. The guilt is gnawing at me like a dog with a bone, and the longer I wait, the worse it feels.

They'll either be proud... or furious that I kept my life from them this long. I'm bracing for both.

Tonight, everyone wanted to hit *The Pocket Lounge*—half club, half dive bar. Dancing, pool tables, neon lights that flicker like a bad memory. Best of both worlds, they said. Of course, I got volunteered as the designated driver, since I don't drink. I couldn't exactly volunteer Simone, since they haven't announced officially yet. I didn't mind. Felt more like gaining three siblings than doing anyone a favor.

Marcus and Joe are cool as hell. The kind of guys you trust instantly without knowing why. Sloane? She's a bombshell with a hurricane in her eyes. The kind of beautiful that ruins you if you're not careful. And then there's London. When we told them our plans, he asked every question a dad would. Safety. Curfew. Who's driving.

Marcus and Joe gave each other a look that said *we clocked that too,* but it wasn't until Mrs. Pierce chimed in—her voice all sing-song sweetness with that cute-as-fuck accent—that they stopped rolling their eyes and actually listened.

Now here I am, parked at the bar nursing a Coke while the others lose themselves on the dance floor, grinding on whoever gets close enough. Three years ago, I would've been in the middle of it. Shirt unbuttoned, hands on hips, chasing the next warm body.

But now?

Now I watch. Now I wait. Not because I'm judging them. Just… because that version of me doesn't live here anymore.

I pull out my phone, aching for Remi. Soon. But not soon enough.

Marley: *I'm sorry for how I've been behaving.*

RLM: *I miss you. I'm sorry for overreacting and accusing you of messing around. I've just had too much time here to think.*

Marley: *I'm telling them tomorrow, and I'm coming to get you. I promise. I'm telling them about the house, you. All of it.*

RLM: *I love you, Mars. So fucking much.*

Marley: *I love you more. I'm so sorry.*

RLM: *It's okay, baby. I understand. I just started to feel insecure. What are you doing right now?*

Marley: *I'm at a bar with Derrick, Simone, and London's sister and brothers. Bored as fuck, thought. What are you doing?*

RLM: Watching porn and playing Sudoku. Are you drinking?

Marley: No, nursing a Coke. Now, about your thing. Is this at the same time? That's some talent.

RLM: It helps me concentrate. Why are you at a bar?

Marley: We finished the welcome dinner and everyone wanted to go out. I'm the designated driver.

RLM: Did your mom have a good time today?

Marley: She did. Dad's here too. That's gonna be a whole fucking thing, but I'll deal with it.

RLM: ….

Marley: Yeah. Exactly. Le sigh. Such is life, I guess. I'll call you when I get back, okay? I love you, Remi.

"Mars?"

The voice snapped my head up. My stomach dipped before my brain even placed it. He looked familiar—too familiar—and the smirk on his face told me he already knew exactly who he was to me.

"Andrew. Andrew Forus."

Fuck this dude. The anger started boiling in my chest immediately at the sound of his name.

"Holy shit, Andy!" I shoved my phone down on the bar, giving a humorless laugh as I pulled him into a quick hug. "How are you, man?"

Poker face at the ready.

"I'm good. I'm good." His eyes raked me up and down in a way that made my stomach knot. He licked his lips, leaning in just enough to make the hairs on my arms stand up. "Fuck,

Mars. You sure have changed a lot since prom. *Fuck.*"

My back went rigid. Heat crawled up the back of my neck as my eyes darted around, scanning the room to see if anyone noticed, if anyone was watching. Especially Derrick. Especially Simone.

I force a grin. The kind I used to wear all the time back home—tight-lipped, teeth barely showing, hiding the urge to punch something behind it.

"Yeah, well. A lot's changed," I say, casual as I can fake. I pick up my glass like it's a lifeline, swirl the ice just to have something in my hands. Something to do besides clench a fist.

He laughs. Loud. Too loud. "You could say that again. I almost didn't recognize you at first—look at you. All filled out. Real grown man shit." He whistles, dragging his eyes down my frame again like I'm something he gets to appraise.

I ease back to put some space between us and laugh again, dry. "Yeah, well. Time and trauma, right?" I raise the glass to my lips, trying to drown the memories that his voice has already unearthed.

Andrew's smirk curved sharper, eyes locking on mine like he was about to drop a grenade.

"Still in the closet, I see." His voice was low, but not low enough, and it hit me like a punch. "Damn. After all these years—and looking as good as you fucking look—you wouldn't even have to try."

My stomach plummeted. My grip on the glass went tight enough to crack it. "Andy—"

He leaned in closer, breath hot against my ear. "What a fucking waste, Mars."

My heart slammed against my ribs. The bar felt suddenly too small, too exposed, like the walls had tilted in on me. My eyes darted across the room again, praying no one had heard, that Derrick wasn't walking up behind me, that no one was looking this way.

I forced a strained laugh, shaking my head. "You really don't know when to shut the fuck up, do you?"

But the way his gaze lingered, hungry and unashamed, told me he had no intention of backing away.

"What, you want to go hide in the back with me again? Tongue-fuck my mouth while your girlfriend waits for you someplace safe?"

The words were poison, slick and loud enough to carry. My chest locked as his eyes shifted over my shoulder, and instinct dragged mine along.

And there they were.

Three familiar faces. The same three assholes from high school leaned back in their seats like nothing had changed, beers in hand, smirks carved across their faces. Watching. Waiting. Laughing.

This was still a fucking game to them. A joke. All of it.

I should've been over it by now, but the memory hit like it was yesterday.

Andrew Forus—he'd been the cute boy since middle school. Pretty green eyes, curly hair that fell into his face, tall and broad-shouldered with a smile sharp enough to cut. And he knew. He knew I liked him. He knew exactly what strings to pull.

The night of prom, he showed up at my house, told me to

meet him out back. I remember the tux strangling me at the collar, the porch light buzzing overhead, the muffled music from inside where my date—Leslie—was waiting for me. He kept stepping closer, grin soft, telling me how good I looked in that suit. How he wanted me to be his first kiss. How he just wanted one moment before the night really started.

And I believed him. God help me, I believed him.

When he kissed me, it was euphoric. My first kiss with a guy—heart in my throat, knees weak, every nerve lit up. Until his hand slid down, grabbed my hard cock, and then his grin turned cruel. "I knew you were a fag."

That's when I saw them. The same three fuckers now smirking across the bar, standing in the corner of my yard that night, laughing while I stood frozen and humiliated.

Andrew leaned in closer now, grin sharp, voice dripping malice. "Oh, come on, Mars. I bet you're hard as a rock right now. Just like prom night."

His hand slid higher up my thigh. The world narrowed.

Red. White. Rage.

Before I could even think better of it, my fist cracked against his jaw. Once. Twice. The satisfying thud of bone against bone rattled up my arm, and he reeled back, blood already blooming from his lip.

His laughter cut off. Chairs scraped. The three guys shot up and stormed across the dance floor like they'd just been waiting for the excuse.

Derrick noticed instantly. He was already moving, shoving through bodies, Simone's voice sharp behind him.

But the first one reached me before Derrick did, throwing

a wild swing. I ducked, came up fast, and drove my fist into his ribs. He folded with a grunt, stumbling sideways into a table that crashed under his weight.

The whole bar shifted around me, music still pounding through the speakers, but every eye turning, the crowd pulling back like they could already sense the storm was about to break and I was right in the middle of it. Joe and Marcus surged forward, shoving people away, and somewhere in the corner of my vision Derrick was dragging Sloane and Simone toward safety.

Then Andrew's fist slammed into my ribs.

The air shot out of me so fast I couldn't even curse, just that raw, gutted silence before the pain hit—sharp and searing, not a clean punch but something that burned like a blade sliding under the skin. I've taken hits before, plenty in the gym, but this one was different. This one hollowed me out.

"Marley!" someone screamed, and the voice cracked through me like a hard wave, too far away, too close, I couldn't tell.

It was hot. Too hot. My shirt clung to me, the club lights smeared into streaks of red and gold, and I tried to laugh, tried to say I was fine, but it came out thin, broken. "I'm okay," I think I said, though my knees gave out before the words even landed, the floor rushing up hard and sticky beneath me.

Fucking hell. One punch and I was wrecked.

"Mars! Call 911! Somebody call 911!" Derrick said this time, his voice was raw and breaking in a way that twisted something in my chest.

I wanted to tell him to shut the hell up, that I could hear

him just fine, that he was making a scene, but then I heard it—his panic cutting deeper.

"There's so much blood. Oh, fuck, there's too much blood! Call my mom!"

Blood? Whose blood? Derrick, are you bleeding?

"Mars, can you hear me?"

Simone? I can hear you.

"Put pressure on it, hold this right here!"

Fuck. Ahh that fucking hurts. He punched the shit out of me.

"It's not working, he's barely breathing!"

"Let them through! Move!"

"Where is that motherfucker?!"

"Derrick! Derrick stop! You're going to kill him!"

Kill who? Why is it so dark in here? I can't see shit. Fuck, my breaths are hard to pull in.

It was too dark, darker than a club should ever be. The edges of everything blurred and folded in, the air thinning, heavy, burning. My chest locked, I couldn't pull breath, couldn't get enough.

Too hot. Too dark. Too quiet.

And then nothing.

19 | JONES

A piercing scream ripped through my sleep, sharp enough to split bone. I shot upright, heart already slamming in my chest.

"Jones—up. Now. We gotta move."

London's voice was ragged, commanding, but all I could hear underneath it was Sev's wails.

She was on the floor, knees buckled, clutching her phone like it was the only thing tethering her to earth. The sound pouring out of her wasn't human—it was feral, grief-wracked, the kind of sound that leaves scars in your marrow.

"Sev!" I jumped up and dropped to her, pulling her into my arms, rocking her, whispering anything, everything. "Hey. Hey, I got you, baby, I got you."

Her body convulsed against mine, the sobs tearing through her chest so violently it made my own ribs ache.

"Lon—" My voice cracked when I looked up, desperate for his eyes, desperate for something steady.

He was yanking shoes on, shoving clothes into a bag with frantic precision. When his gaze met mine, it was already wet, already broken.

"Marley was stabbed, Jones." His words landed like gunfire. "At the bar." He presses his thumbs into his eyes and takes a deep breath. "They're doing CPR. He doesn't have a pulse."

The breath was torn clean out of me. A hollowing. A void.

Sev went boneless in my arms, and I clutched her tighter, as if I let go even for a second she'd shatter into a million pieces on the floor. My throat burned, vision blurred, but I forced my voice steady.

"Bring her clothes," I barked, even as my own voice shook. "I'll dress her in the truck."

London nodded once, sharp, already moving. I lifted Sev into my arms, her cries muffling into my chest, her fists clutching at my shirt like she could hold the world together if she just gripped hard enough.

And all I could think, through the roar in my skull, was that I couldn't lose him. Not like this. Not tonight.

The drive blurred—sirens in my head though none trailed us, the silence inside the truck broken only by Sev whispering Marley's name. Over and over, like a prayer. Like a curse. I sat in the back with her, dressing her like she was a child. She was boneless in my arms, pliant, empty. Every movement felt wrong, like I was piecing together a broken doll.

When we pulled up to the hospital, she bolted. I'd never seen her move so fast—hair flying, feet slapping pavement, like sheer will might drag her boy back to life.

The waiting room hit like a scene from a nightmare. Sloane and Simone huddled together in the corner, red-eyed and shaking. London went straight for them. Joe and Marcus sat nearby, knuckles swollen, faces bruised, their silence heavier than the antiseptic stink clinging to the air.

But it was Derrick that stopped me cold. That stopped *her*.

He was pacing in frantic circles, shirt soaked crimson, hands and chin smeared with blood. His eyes were bloodshot, wild, muttering words that tumbled too fast to catch.

The moment he saw Sev, he broke. He fell to his knees, arms clinging to her waist, his face pressed to her stomach like he was a child again. "They got his pulse back on the way here," he sobbed, every word cracking. "But he was dead, Mom. He was fucking dead. And I—I couldn't stop it. I couldn't help him."

Her hands cradled his face, her own tears blinding her, but she didn't collapse. She couldn't. She had one son on the floor and another fighting for his life behind sterile walls.

"Where are the fuckers that attacked him?" London's voice cut through the chaos, sharp, lethal.

"Two were arrested," Simone said, her voice thin but steady. "The third guy is here. In ICU. He didn't walk away clean." She looked at Derrick then, her own tears spilling fast. "Ricky…he almost killed him. I'm not sure he didn't. When the EMTs started CPR on Mars—he went after him."

The silence that followed was jagged, the kind that says someone's already broken past the point of no return.

Hours bled together. Every doctor who came through the double doors was an empty promise, hope rising in Sev's eyes only to shatter with a shake of the head. Me and London did what we could—coffee, blankets, anything to keep her anchored. She drifted between my lap and his, clinging like she might float away if one of us let go. Every few minutes, she whispered Marley's name under her breath. Breathing. Waiting. Breaking.

Derrick was a live wire. His knee bounced nonstop, jaw clenched so tight I thought his teeth might crack. Every so often, his gaze cut toward a guy in the corner. Big, broad-shouldered, quiet. He hadn't moved in hours, just sat there like a shadow. Watching.

Finally, Derrick snapped. He shot to his feet, rage propelling him forward. "Who the fuck are you?" His voice cracked across the waiting room. "You've been sitting here this entire time, just watching us. Are you related to that asshole who stabbed my brother? Huh? You family to that piece of shit?"

Chairs scraped. Me, Marcus and Joe—we were all moving at once to intercept, to stop him from throwing the first punch.

The guy stood. And Christ, he was massive. He had at least three, maybe four inches on Derrick's six-two frame, built like someone who knew his way around a weight rack. But he didn't square up. He didn't so much as flinch.

Instead, he lifted his hands, palms out, voice low but steady. "Derrick. No." His eyes were bloodshot, his nose raw like he'd been wiping it too often. He looked just as wrung out as the rest of us. "I'm not related to that fucker."

Derrick froze mid-step, chest heaving, fists flexing like he was deciding whether to swing, anyway.

The man swallowed, shoulders tight, but his hand didn't

waver. "My name's Remi," he said. His voice cracked halfway through. "I'm… I'm a friend of your brother's."

Remi…

Wait…*that's* Remi?! Remi is a…*man?*

"Bullshit," Derrick snapped. "Who called you? We don't fucking know you. How did you even know he was here?"

By now, all of us were on our feet. The waiting room felt like an interrogation room, the fluorescent lights buzzing, every eye locked on this stranger.

"The hospital called me."

The words dropped like stones. Silence stretched, taut as a tripwire.

Derrick's nostrils flared. "Who. The *fuck.* Are you." His patience was a match head, seconds from striking flame.

The man exhaled slowly, like he'd been waiting for this exact moment. He lowered himself back into his chair with a composure that only made it sting more, crossing one ankle over his knee. When he looked up, his gaze was steady—too steady.

"I'm his emergency contact."

The floor tilted. No one spoke.

"My name is Remilee Monroe." He folded his hands in his lap, calm as anything, though the tension in his jaw betrayed him. "If you need more information than that, you'll have to wait until Marley wakes up. It's not my story to tell."

"You son of a—" Derrick started forward, but before he could finish, a voice cut through the room.

"Moore family?"

Every head snapped toward the doorway. A doctor stood there in scrubs, mask hanging at his neck, clipboard under his arm, expression steady but carved in fatigue.

"Yes. Yes, that's us." Half of us answered at once, voices tripping over each other like we could will his next words into being good ones.

He stepped closer, tone brisk but clear. "I'm Dr. Roderick, Marley's attending. He lost a significant amount of blood. He coded once at the bar and again in the ambulance, but both times we got him back quickly. He's stable now. The wound has been repaired; he received a transfusion, and he's awake. *Weak*, but alert. We'll keep him in ICU tonight, move him to a regular room tomorrow if his numbers hold. If recovery stays on track, he could be discharged in twenty-four to forty-eight hours."

Sev sagged against London, a sob tearing free, and for the first time in hours, the air in the room wasn't razor-sharp—it broke, shuddered, filled with relief.

"You can see him now," Dr. Roderick added, flipping a page on the clipboard. "But only one or two at a time. Which one of you is his husband?"

All eyes shifted. The stranger in the corner—big, red-eyed, carrying weight none of us understood—stood slowly, hands fisted at his sides. "That's me."

The doctor nodded and extended a bag of Marley's belongings. "He's been asking for you. I'll take you back to him now."

The room erupted in silence—thick, choking, stunned.

Derrick's face snapped toward Mom like she'd have the answers. Simone's hand flew to her mouth. Joe and Marcus both froze mid-breath. London went stone still, his arm tightening around Sev as if he could hold her together through the shatter.

And Sev? She just stared, eyes wide and glassy, her lips parting around words that refused to come.

Three years ago...

It's been six months since Derrick's wedding, and this is my first time out of the house doing anything remotely 'fun', and I can't even muster the energy to hang with my friends. I'm trying to pull myself out of this funk, but I just feel like I'm wading through water every day.

"Hi, Mrs. Marulli," I called, leaning against the doorframe of my roommate's parents' kitchen.

She turned, spoon in hand, eyes crinkling. "Hey there, Marls. What are you doing in here, love? Go hang out with the gang."

My roommate, Mace Marulli, was graduating, and his whole senior class had decided to throw one last blowout before the real world came calling. All of us undergrads were invited, but a college party wasn't exactly my scene—not since I'd sworn off alcohol.

I shrugged, offering her a tired smile. "Just needed a breather. Thought I'd come to find the only sane person in this house."

She chuckled softly, returning to her sauce-stirring duties. "I'm flattered. But I'm guessing it's not just the crowd getting to you."

Leave it to a mother to see right through me.

I leaned farther against the frame, arms crossed tight over my chest. "It's been… a year."

Her eyes met mine again, this time with a softness that hit too close. "I know it has, sweetheart."

I swallowed hard and looked down at my shoes. I didn't want to cry in her kitchen. I didn't want to feel anything, really. Not grief. Not guilt. Not the familiar shame that crept in when I thought about how long I'd let myself drift like this.

While the guys were out there drinking, grinding, and shouting lyrics they didn't even know, I'd found myself drifting toward the kitchen. Watching his mom work was like watching a conductor at her peak—stirring, chopping, sliding trays in and out of the oven without missing a beat. It reminded me of Mom and Jones in the kitchen back home: that wordless rhythm, the one that felt like love in motion.

It was chaos, sure, but the good kind. Organized chaos. And definitely not what you'd expect for a backyard kegger. Pans hissed, knives flashed, and the air smelled like it belonged in a five-star restaurant. She wasn't cooking for drunk twenty-somethings—she was cooking like Michelin inspectors were sitting in the dining room.

"Not really my scene," I said, shrugging as I crossed my arms. "Need a hand?"

Her laugh was warm and just a little teasing as she wiped her small hands on a fall-themed apron. "Got any kitchen skills, or do I need to stick you on potato-peeling duty?"

She gave the sauce a stir, lifted the spoon to her lips, and frowned—like it had personally offended her mother.

I rubbed the back of my neck, nerves climbing. "I mean… I've done some cooking. Nothing professional, of course."

"Here." She dipped the spoon again and held it out to me. "Tell me what's missing. I've made this damn sauce a million times, but something's off."

I leaned forward, lips parting around the spoon. The flavor hit instantly—silky, saffron-tinged, but… hollow. It had all the right notes, but none of the soul.

"It's good," I said carefully, keeping my face neutral even as my instincts argued otherwise.

Her eyes narrowed. She caught it instantly and laughed, shaking her head. "Don't bullshit me, kid. It's missing something."

She turned toward the sink, and I realized she was about to dump the whole pan.

"Wait—don't." The words leaped out before I could stop them. My heart was pounding so loud it nearly drowned my voice. "I don't know what I'm talking about, but… my family cooks. I've been watching them my whole life."

I exhaled, trying to steady myself. "It tastes like… you used chicken stock instead of fish stock. Is this supposed to be a saffron velouté?"

Her brows shot up, impressed despite herself. "It is."

"Then…" My throat went dry, but I pushed through. "Maybe it just needs a hit of acid. Lemon zest, maybe yuzu if you've got it. Or even a quick white wine reduction."

For a moment she just stared, spoon suspended midair. Then that grin bloomed—slow, knowing, like she'd just uncovered a secret ingredient she hadn't known she was missing.

"Well, I'll be damned. Look at you, Chef Marley. That was impressive as hell. I'm pissed at myself for grabbing the wrong stock, but you just saved me a shit-ton of rework."

And there it was. The first flicker of something that felt like more than being Sevynn Moore's son.

She opened the drawer beside the pantry and tossed me an apron, jerking her chin toward the counter. "Come on then, Chef. You've earned yourself a spot on the line."

I caught it midair and slipped it on—only to hear her snort. When I looked up, her cheeks were pink, and she was doing a poor job of hiding her grin.

"What?" I asked, glancing down.

The apron read, in bold red letters: *I like my meat thick and juicy.*

My face went nuclear. I ran a hand through my hair, muttering, "Of course it does."

She was outright laughing now, hand over her mouth.

"Put me to work, Mrs. Marulli," I said, deadpan, tugging the apron strings tight. "And we never, ever talk about this again."

I spent the next two hours at her side—tasting, chopping,

adjusting. Every time she asked my opinion, my stomach tied itself in knots, but I answered anyway. And damned if her eyes didn't light up every single time I was right.

When Mr. Marulli came in, he kissed her cheek and murmured something about guests arriving. She bent to whisper in his ear, and his gaze shifted to me — a twenty-year-old undergrad standing a little too close to his wife's saucepans. He gave me a long once-over, unreadable, and walked out without a word.

Uneasy didn't even begin to cover it.

"Uh… thanks, Mrs. Marulli, for letting me help," I said, already halfway to the door. "I should probably go."

She waved me off with a smile. "Good. Go hang out, enjoy being twenty-something — it's gone in a blink. And thank you for saving my velouté."

But I didn't go hang with the guys. I walked straight out of that house convinced I'd overstepped — that I'd just embarrassed myself in front of people who actually knew what they were doing.

Turns out, I hadn't screwed up at all.

Mrs. Marulli told her husband how I'd stood beside her all night, how I'd caught the mistake, how I "had a palate." The next morning, Mr. Marulli called. Asked me to come meet him at one of his restaurants.

That meeting turned into an internship.
The internship turned into twelve-hour shifts — busting my ass, soaking up everything I could, sneaking in recipe ideas when no one was looking.

Some of those recipes are still used now across five of his

eight restaurants.

So when he offered me head chef, I asked him point-blank, "Is this because I'm Sevynn Moore's kid?"

He stared at me like I'd just insulted his mother. "Marley, I didn't know you were her kid until you said it just now. I don't make it my business to know other restaurant owners' lives. You work for me, you earn it by grit and merit. I don't give a fuck who your mother is."

That should've been the end of it. Should've been the moment I finally stepped out of her shadow.

But the kitchen wasn't easy—namely because of Remilee Monroe.

And boy, did he make my life a living hell that first month.

Tonight, the kitchen buzzed; knives on boards, pans hissing, servers popping in and out like they owned the place. My first week wearing the title *Head Chef*, and the weight of it sat squarely on my shoulders.

"Fire table six!" I called, plating the duck. "Two medium, one rare, sides up in three."

"Yes, Chef," the line echoed. All except one.

Remilee Monroe leaned back against his station, arms crossed, smirk sharp enough to slice through steel. He'd been Senior Sous for years, practically running the kitchen whenever Chef Marulli wasn't around. Everyone knew it. *He* knew it. And now, suddenly, he was answering to me.

"Problem, Remi?" I asked, voice steady even though my blood was humming.

He shrugged, slow. "Just funny how fast some people climb.

Some of us bleed for years on this line, but hey — guess it helps to have a famous last name."

The words hit like a slap. The kitchen went quiet for a beat, every set of eyes flicking between us.

Before I could answer, Chef Marulli — who'd been walking the pass — set his spoon down with a little too much force. The clang made Remi flinch.

"Careful, Monroe." His voice was calm, but his eyes weren't. "Don't mistake grit for nepotism. I promoted Chef Moore because he earned it. You don't like it, you know where the door is."

The air crackled. I held Remi's stare, unblinking. He held it right back, jaw tight, but said nothing.

"Table six, Chef," I reminded him, the corner of my mouth tugging just slightly.

He turned back to his station, muttering a clipped, "Yes, Chef," under his breath.

But the fire in his eyes said this was far from over.

Except it didn't stay fire.

That summer became a blur of heat, steel, and noise — and somewhere in that chaos, I found my purpose. Over the next few weeks, something shifted. Maybe it was the pressure of service, maybe it was just survival — but the heat between us stopped being combative. We weren't locking horns over missed garnishes or mistimed sears anymore. Instead, we found a rhythm.

His knife passed me herbs before I even asked. My hand slid a pan onto his flame before he reached for it. One move fed the next.

Like the kitchen itself had decided to stop fighting us and force us into sync.

It wasn't friendship—not yet. But it wasn't war either.

"Come grab a beer with me, Moore," Remi called one night as we trudged toward the parking lot, our shirts damp with sweat, the scent of garlic and grease still clinging to our skin.

I glanced at my phone. "Bars are closed, Monroe… and I don't drink."

He smirked, leaning back against his car like the whole damn world could wait. "I've got a bar at my place. Top-shelf Pepsi. Come on. It was a shit night."

I blinked. Because this wasn't a dare. Wasn't a jab. This was something else. An invitation—clean and quiet.

And maybe it was the low hum of exhaustion or the way his voice curved around the word *come*, but for the first time, I really *saw* him.

Taller than me by a good four inches. Built like a fucking Viking—broad chest, thick arms, a dark beard that tapered into a neat point. His hair was tied back, the sides shaved clean, a soft contrast to the sharp line of his jaw. Those green eyes didn't just look at you. They saw through shit. And right then, they were fixed on me.

Remi Monroe was beautiful.

And somehow, I'd missed that—until the moment I didn't.

"Fuck, Remi." I breathed, taking in his space around me. "This is where you *live*?"

The apartment was way nicer than I expected. High ceilings, big windows spilling light across exposed brick, the kind of old floors that creak when you move but somehow make it feel like the place has seen things. It wasn't just stylish — it had soul.

And in the corner? A full bar setup that looked like it belonged in a high-end lounge. He wasn't kidding. Except for the Pepsi. That was straight-up regular fucking Pepsi, the liar.

He poured himself a bourbon, then handed me a glass. "Your Top-Shelf Pepsi on the Rocks, Chef."

I rolled my eyes but took it, settling onto the leather stool he nodded toward. I should've felt uneasy. Out of place. But I didn't.

"So," he said, lowering himself onto the stool beside me, "I owe you an apology, Monroe."

My brows rose. That wasn't what I expected. "Yeah?"

"Yeah." He took a slow sip, eyes on the glass. "I've been a dick to you since day one, but you know your shit."

He shook his head, chuckling — that low, rough sound that somehow crawled right under my skin. "Like, you *really* fucking know your shit. Color me impressed, Moore."

"Wow. That, uh…" I fumbled, feeling the heat crawl up my neck. "Thanks."

From there, the conversation just… flowed. We talked about the line, about the pressure, about nothing and everything in between.

When I finally glanced at the clock, it was five in the morning. Three hours—gone like smoke.

He leaned in, bourbon still rough in his voice. "I'm going to kiss you now, Moore."

His eyes stayed locked on mine—steady, unflinching. "You've got five seconds to tell me no."

My pulse thundered in my ears. I didn't say no.

We were both off the next day, so after a few hours of sleep—him in his bed, me on the couch—we went to breakfast. Talked more. Kissed more. Touched more.

Two weeks later, I was already in love with him. I didn't even see it happening; I just looked up one night and realized the ground beneath me had shifted, and he was the reason.

It took three months before I worked up the nerve to let him all the way in, and when we finally had sex, it wasn't the awkward scramble I'd always dreaded. It was patient. Intentional. Like he'd been waiting his whole life for me to catch up. Every step, every boundary, was mine to set. He made damn sure of it.

And he didn't just love me—he loved a version of me I hadn't known existed. A version that wanted to try. To commit. To be better.

So why the hell didn't I tell my family?

Because it was easier not to.

I love them—God, I love them with everything in me—but Derrick's always been the golden son. The achiever. The one they brag about at dinner parties.
Me? I was the screw-up. The one they loved in that complicated, worried way. The kind of love that comes with a sigh.

I didn't want to hand them another piece of myself just so they could wait for the other shoe to drop.
I wanted to be proud of what I'd built—without their doubt

hanging over it.

Eighteen months ago, I asked Remi to marry me. We flew to Vegas and did it that same night. No planning. No big moment. Just us.

Eight months ago, we closed on our first house. And the very next morning, we adopted Brutus—a scrappy little blonde Yorkie who looks like a lion but yaps like a squeaky toy.

That's my life. *Our* life.

An entire world I built in New Orleans.

A life I'm not failing at.

A life I'm not fucking up.

"You know… this need of yours for attention is reaching dangerous heights, Mars."

Remi's voice tugged me out of the haze before I even opened my eyes. My lips twitched into the ghost of a smile. "Hi, baby."

When I blinked, the room into focus, the world was too white, too sterile—beeping machines, the sterile sting of antiseptic, the heavy drag of an IV in my arm. My throat was raw, every breath like swallowing glass. And then there was him.

My Remi.

He walked in slowly, like each step cost him. Shoulders tight, jaw locked, eyes red-rimmed as if he'd been holding back the whole world for hours. He couldn't even meet my gaze at first, staring at the floor like if he looked at me full-on, he'd break apart.

I shifted against the stiff hospital sheets, wincing at the pull in my side. "You look like hell," I rasped, my voice wrecked from the tube they must've shoved down my throat.

That finally pulled his eyes to mine. God, the way he looked at me. Just… relief. And love, so heavy it nearly pinned me to the bed. He dropped into the chair beside me, exhaling like he'd been holding his breath for three years straight.

"You scared the shit out of me," he said, low and rough.

"Don't you ever fucking do that again."

I let out a dry laugh that scraped my lungs. "Getting stabbed wasn't exactly on my to-do list." My hand shifted, weak, but I found his and curled my fingers around it. "They know, don't they?"

His silence was answer enough. His thumb pressed into my palm like he was anchoring me down.

"Fuck," I whispered. My chest ached worse than the stitches. "My mom?"

Remi swallowed, finally leaning close enough that his forehead brushed mine. "She's outside. So is Derrick. Simone. All of them. Jones too." He pulled back enough to search my face, eyes still wet. "The doctor told them I was your husband. Because I am. And Marley, I'm not sorry about it. I know you wanted to do this in your time, but the universe had other plans."

My heart stumbled in my chest—weak, stitched-up, but somehow it still managed a wild kick.

"I don't want you to be sorry," I said, my voice cracking on it. "I just… fuck, Rem. I wanted to tell them my way. I wanted to tell them when I wasn't bleeding all over a bar floor."

Remi's laugh was broken glass. He kissed my knuckles and shook his head. "Yeah, well. You Moore boys never do anything easy."

Despite the pain, despite the wires and the IV and the fact that I'd technically died twice tonight, I felt it—the tiniest smile tugging at my lips. "Yeah… we really don't."

"Derrick thought I was related to the guy that hurt you." Remi's mouth tugged into the faintest smirk, though his eyes were still raw. "He was ready to fight me in the middle of the waiting room. Full-on Moore temper, fists and all."

I groaned, half a laugh breaking out of me even though it burned like hell in my ribs. "Sounds about right. He probably would've broken his hand on your jaw."

"Maybe," Remi said, leaning back just enough to look at me properly, his thumb still stroking over my palm. Then he added, "Also… you didn't tell me Jones was that hot. I feel even more jealous now."

That pulled a sharper laugh out of me, even though it ended in a cough. "Remi—Jesus. I get stabbed, die twice, and you're in here worried about Jones being hot?"

"I'm just saying," he shrugged, feigning nonchalance even as his lips twitched. "Tall. Cocky. That scruffy thing he's got going on? Dangerous combo. You could've warned me before I walked into the waiting room looking like the tragic, less-attractive husband."

I squeezed his hand, weak but deliberate. "Shut up. You're not less anything. You're the one I chose." My voice cracked at the end, but the truth in it was steady. "Jones is… Jones. My family's person. But you're mine. You're way fucking hotter, have you seen you. My viking king."

The smirk dropped right off his face, replaced with something that made my throat go tight. He leaned in, pressing his lips to my forehead—soft, reverent.

"God, Mars," he whispered, forehead resting against mine like he was afraid I'd vanish if he let go. "Don't ever scare me like that again."

"I'm really sorry," I rasped, my throat tight. "I had you

stashed at a hotel like some dirty secret while I sat here too chicken-shit to tell my family. I should've just brought you with me, day one."

His thumb brushed across my knuckles, steady as ever. "Hey. Look at me." I did, and there it was—those eyes that never flinched, never judged. "You don't need to apologize. You gotta do this in your own time, Mars. Nobody else gets to set the pace for you. I'm sorry I started being a dick about it."

"I made you sit there alone. In some random hotel room."

"And I survived." His mouth curved finally. "Porn and Sudoku kept me busy."

"You're the worst."

"And yet, you married me." He leaned in, kissing me quick and careful. "Rest. I'm not going anywhere."

My eyes closed, the weight of his words sinking into me. My family knows...

The sound of whispers pulls me from sleep. Soft, urgent. Like they're trying not to wake the dead.

My eyes flutter open.

This isn't the same room.

It's bigger. Quieter. The air feels more still. Sterile, but... gentler somehow.

Remi's passed out on the couch—legs hanging off the edge, arms folded across his chest like he fell asleep mid-sentence. I track the voices and find them—Mom, Dad, Jones, London, and Derrick—clustered near the foot of the bed with the doctor. They're speaking low, heads bowed like they're in a church pew. I can't make out the words.

Then I see it—Derrick. His shirt is stained dark and tacky with blood.

My stomach drops.

What the fuck happened that night?

Mom glances over, and her hand flies to her mouth. A gasp escapes—sharp, shattered—then a sob, broken wide open.

"Hi, baby," she cries, but she doesn't move toward me. None of them do. Not yet.

They're frozen, like I'm something fragile.

"Hi," I croak, throat dry and cracking. I try again. "Hey."

"Fuck." The word slips from Derrick like a punch to the gut. He drops into the chair across from the bed, buries his face in his hands—and cries. Jones rubs his shoulder, his own jaw clenched.

"How are you feeling, son?" Dad asks, voice tight.

Movement pulls my attention—Remi. He jerks upright on the couch like he forgot where he was, like he only just realized the room isn't empty anymore. His eyes widen when he sees everyone.

Yeah, dude. *Excellent job keeping watch.*

"I'll give you all some privacy," he says, already pushing to his feet.

Dad's gaze lands on him—and sweet *hell*, his eyes go *bug-wide* like Remi's a damn giant who wandered in from the woods. It would be funny if it weren't *us.*

"Remi," I rasp, "wait. Stay. Please."

He pauses. Looks at me. Not the others—*me.* And there it is, that unspoken check-in. *You sure?* One word in a look.

I nod.

He sits again, back straight, hands folded between his knees. He's trying to take up less space than a man his size can, but it's not possible. He's just *there*—solid, unflinching, like he always is when I need him.

"I'm okay," I say finally, though I'm not sure I believe it. "Sorry for all of this, Mom… London." The shame's already crawling in under my skin, burrowing deep. Ruining their wedding week. Their *moment.* Of course I did.

"Don't you *fucking dare* say that, Marley." London's voice cuts through the room like a whip, and I blink—because he's never raised it at me. Not once.

That's when I notice the tears slipping down his face while he stares straight at me, fierce as hell.

"Me nor your mom gives *two fucks* about that wedding. You are the most important thing. Nothing else. *You understand me?*"

Damn. *Okay, then.*

"Yes, sir." I whisper, fighting back tears.

He crosses the room without hesitation and presses a kiss to my temple, hand bracing the side of my face.

"I love you, my boy."

Mom's hand wraps gently around my foot, rubbing slow

and soft, tears sliding silently down her cheeks as she nods.

"Is there something you want to tell us, honey?" she asks, her voice quiet—careful. It's not lost on me that she keeps glancing at Remi, side-eye full of questions.

It's awkward as hell. But here we go.

"Yeah." I lean my head back against the pillow, take a deep breath. "I'm gay," I say, steadying my nerves as the words land. "I met Remi at LeVeaux."

No one explodes. No one even flinches.

So I keep going.

"We got married a year and a half ago—the night I got promoted."

That one hits harder. Mouths drop open. Sadness sweeps through the room like a breeze through a cracked window. Realization—and a kind of grief. Like they're looking at someone they don't quite recognize. Someone they missed.

"We, uh…" I glance at Remi, who gives me a small nod—solid, grounding. "We closed on our home eight months ago. We have a dog named Brutus. I've done well in stocks—built a cushion so we're comfortable. I'm working with Chef LeVeaux to open a sister branch called LeFèvre in New Orleans, where I'll be part owner. We break ground next month, riding the Michelin-star momentum for publicity."

I rattle it all off too fast—like if I stop, I might shove it all back down again. I don't want to. I want everything on the table.

But the room goes still.

Everyone is staring at me.

Then—Mom moves. She walks over to Remi, her hands shaking slightly as she reaches out.

"I'm Sevynn," she says. "You can call me Sev."

Her voice cracks with restrained tears, but she meets his eyes. She *sees* him. And maybe, in that moment, she sees me too.

"Remilee Monroe," he says gently, taking her hand—but then, being Remi, he pulls her into a hug that swallows her whole.

One by one, they follow. Derrick. Jones. London. Each of them gets swept up in one of Remi's bear hugs. And despite how big he is—how *intimidating* he looks—they're going to see what I see. The teddy bear. The goofball. The man who made a home out of me.

I realized a moment too late that Dad hadn't moved. While everyone else made their way to Remi, he tucked himself into a corner, arms folded, jaw tight. The look on his face? I knew it too well.

This—*this* was the reason I'd kept my distance. This moment right here would decide the shape of my future with him.

"Dad?" I ask, voice tight. Hopeful, but barely.

He doesn't move. Just shakes his head slowly.

"I can see the headlines now. *Jaxon Moore's son, gay.*" His voice is flat. Disgusting. "Fuck, Marley. This is the life you choose to live? After everything you've accomplished, you throw it away for some silly *lifestyle* choice?"

The words land like soot in my mouth. I feel the tears well before I can stop them, my heart collapsing in on itself. I knew.

Deep down, I always *knew* he wouldn't accept me. But knowing doesn't soften the blow.

Before I can even open my mouth, a chair flies—*flies*—across the room and crashes into the wall just inches from his head.

"Get the *fuck* out of my son's hospital room." London's voice is thunder. Controlled, but barely. "Walk the fuck out, Jaxon. And I mean right the fuck now."

Dad turns, mouth opening to retort—but London moves.

He *rushes* him.

Doesn't touch him, doesn't have to. The force of his fury is enough to rattle the windows. A growl—*feral, low, unrecognizable*—rips from his throat, and the room stills around it.

"*Out.*" London snarls. He's shaking with anger.

Dad flinches like he's been slapped. And in that moment, he knows.

He *knows* he's fucked up beyond repair. He turns and walks out without another word. But the damage is already done.

I break. A sob tears through me, loud and uncontrollable. I hadn't realized—until this very second—how badly I still wanted him to love me. To choose me. To see me and *stay*.

And now? Now I know for certain, he never will.

This is not the time to be sporting a hard cock, but holy fucking hell—*Unleashed* London is unlike anything I've ever seen.

That fury… that *feral devotion*… it lit the whole damn room on fire.

The moment Jax walks out, London's arms are around Marley. No hesitation. No questions. He wraps his whole body around his head like he can shield him from the damage, like if he holds tight enough, none of it will stick.

Sevynn had bolted after Jax. Her face—fuck. I'd never seen her look like that. Not even when she was burying her mother. Her back was stiff as steel, but her shoulders were shaking. I can hear her sobbing down the hall. She's not chasing to forgive. She's chasing to finish this. To cut him loose. I saw the straw snap in her eyes before she turned. Whatever tether she'd clung to for all these years? It broke clean.

Derrick sat next to me, bent over like he was praying or trying not to fall apart, his hands knotted against his forehead.

And Remi—Remi hadn't moved. Just sat with his elbows on his knees, staring at the floor like it might open up and give him something to fix.

"Don't you cry for that bastard. You are loved," London says, voice thick with tears. "Just as you fucking are. By everyone who matters."

Marley's hands fist London's shirt, and he cries so hard it hurts.

"I know, son," London whispers, breaking right along with him. "*Fuck*, I know."

I step out of the room before I lose it—before I do something reckless. My chest feels too tight to hold the air in. I want to scream for Marley, scream into the fucking universe that he deserved *better* than what Jax just gave him.

But then I see her.

Sev.

She's leaning against the wall, shoulders hunched, tears streaming down her face in silent, steady rivers. Her head is bowed, but I can feel the weight she's holding just by looking at her.

I walk over without a word and pull her into my arms.

Her eyes fly open, startled, breath catching in her throat like she forgot how to take one.

"Shhh," I murmur, pressing a kiss to her forehead. My voice is barely holding. "You're okay. I've got you."

She clings tighter, her body trembling. And for a moment, there's nothing else. No hallway. No hospital. Just the shaking woman in my arms and the blood in my ears pounding with everything I couldn't say back in that room.

"I don't know him, Jones," she sobs. "My own son is a stranger to me. Married? He's been hiding his entire life from us." Her voice cracks on the last word, and it shatters something in me.

I pull her tighter, resting my chin on top of her head.

"He just wanted to make you proud." I take a breath, rubbing slow circles along her back. "He wasn't trying to shut you out of his life, Sev. I think… he just wanted to remodel the place before he let you back in."

She lets out a sound—half laugh, half sob—and buries her face deeper into my chest.

After a moment, I ask gently, "What did you say to Jax?"

"God!" she explodes, pulling back just enough to angrily wipe her tears with shaking hands. "I'm so fucking furious with him." Her voice cracks. "I told him to never contact us again. That was it. That *was it*. He will never be able to hurt my boys like that again. I don't care that they're grown men. I won't have it. Not ever again."

"Ms. Washington?" Remi's voice cuts through the hallway like a sonic boom.

He's so fucking intimidating, it's insane.

Sev startles, quickly wiping at her tears. "Hi, Remi." Her voice is sheepish, tired. "Sorry about all of this. I can't imagine what you must be thinking."

"No, please." He steps forward, gently taking her hands in his. She has to crane her neck to meet his gaze—hell, *so do I*.

"I just wanted to say I'm sorry," he says with a calm none

of us are feeling. "To you. To all of you, really." He glances at me, then back to Sev. "This secrecy—it was never about keeping you out of Marley's life. I didn't mean to eavesdrop, but I heard what you said to Jones."

"Then why?" Her hands fall away from his as she steps back, arms crossing like she's trying to hold herself together. "You've been married for a year and a half. His job, the house, the star, all of it was kept from us."

Her breath hitches. "I'm his mother, Remi. And I know nothing about who that man is in there." She presses a trembling hand to her chest. "I love him no less... but he's a stranger to me."

Remi's face softens with remorse. The kind that sits heavy in a man's chest because he knows this wound has his name on it, too.

"Because he didn't want you to worry," Remi says quietly, but with the weight of someone who's heard this from Marley in a dozen different ways before now. "He wanted to show you he had made it. Not ask you to watch him struggle to get there."

He takes a breath, eyes shining now. "You're not the reason he kept it from you. You're the reason he worked so damn hard to have something worth showing. Your son is the most driven and hard-working man I know. And it's my understanding that hasn't always been the case, he wanted to come to you with diamonds, not coal."

"I can understand that," Sev says softly, almost like she's speaking more to herself than anyone else. "It's just… a lot. All at once. He hasn't been home since Derrick's wedding. I went to see him and he introduced me to a girlfriend." Her voice cracks slightly. "And then I find out about you."

"That was my sister you met," Remi says, voice gentle, steady. "He wasn't ready yet. I know it's hurtful. But he didn't mean for it to be cruel."

Sev nods, eyes rimmed red, but a small smile manages to fight its way to the surface. "I look forward to getting to know you, Remi. Both of you."

She steps forward and pulls him into a hug. This time, he doesn't resist. You can actually see it—the way his whole body exhales tension. The way he melts into her embrace is like he's been waiting for this moment longer than he'd admit.

When they pull apart, Sev wipes her cheeks and heads back into Marley's room ahead of us. A second later, a shriek rings out.

"Derrick!"

We rounded the corner just in time to find Derrick fully sprawled in the hospital bed—under the covers—with Marley. His arm is tucked under Marley's head like a human pillow. It's oddly gentle for a grown-ass man invading another grown-ass man's space.

"I'm not moving," Derrick grumbles, voice muffled against Marley's head. "Not happening."

Marley blinks, clearly too stunned to form words, and London just stands there with his mouth slightly open like he walked into the Twilight Zone.

"This is a new level of weird, even for you, Ricky," London mutters.

Derrick smirks, eyes closed, already half-asleep. "Yeah, well. Love makes you do strange shit."

"Is he always like this?" Remi asks, chuckling low in his chest as he watches Derrick settle in like he pays rent.

"Yes, brother-in-law," Derrick mumbles without missing a beat, eyes still closed. "I am. Get used to it. Also…" He lifts one finger in the air, like a final decree before sleep claims him. "We need to have a very serious discussion about your beard after my nap. It's immaculate. Like, magazine-cover immaculate."

Remi blinks, caught between amusement and confusion. "Did he just compliment me and threaten me at the same time?"

"Yup," Marley mutters, still stuck in the same position Derrick pulled him into. "Welcome to the family."

"I don't need to be carried into the house, Derrick."

It's been four days since the stabbing, and apparently, I've lost all credibility when it comes to walking upright. This man—this absolute menace—has insisted on carrying me bridal-style like I'm some Victorian damsel instead of someone with fully functioning legs and a fresh scar.

He just smirks down at me. "That's cute. You thinking your opinion matters right now."

Derrick's been a new brand of weird since everything happened. Tender in bursts. Unhinged the rest of the time. I haven't decided if I'm grateful or emotionally unstable by osmosis.

The truth is, it *has* been beautiful. Four days of quiet. Of family. Of healing.

Remi and London bonded like long-lost brothers, all brooding glares and protective instincts, like they were separated at birth by different action franchises. Remi and Mom talked for hours—recipes, restaurants, spice blends—and she not-so-subtly offered us both jobs at the new place she's opening. She wants us to move here. Permanently.

Derrick and Simone made a decision too. They're building a house on the back lot—close enough for morning coffee and impulsive dinners, far enough for the illusion of privacy. They haven't told anyone why yet. Not out loud. But I know. They want the baby close to Mom and London. They're waiting to share it, letting the rest of us have our moment first.

And now? Now I'm being carried across the threshold like we're on the cover of a Nicholas Sparks book.

"I can walk," I mutter again, but I don't push him away.

"Uh huh," Derrick says, not breaking stride. "And I can *not* be the sexiest man in this family, but here we are."

I narrow my eyes at the smug bastard. "I can tell you're struggling by the red creeping up your neck. There's a little vein right there," I poke it with my finger, "that's about to burst."

"Well, you're the one who gained fifty fucking pounds."

"I'm going to hurt you if you drop him, Derrick Moore!" Mom yells from behind us, her voice a mix of panic and maternal threat.

He snorts but holds me tighter, exaggerated like I'm made of glass. "Yes, ma'am," he mutters.

The house greets us with the rich smell of maple syrup and coffee, warm and familiar and mouthwatering. My stomach growls so loud that Derrick actually looks down at me in concern.

"I think your spleen just asked for a pancake."

But when we round the corner into the kitchen, we stop cold.

It isn't London's mom at the stove. It's Jessica.

She's standing there, apron tied clumsily around her waist, Lillian balanced on her hip. The little one is babbling and chewing on what looks like a measuring spoon, completely unaware of the tension that's just crash-landed in the doorway.

Jessica's smile falters. "Hey," she says softly, tentatively. "I didn't know you'd be back already. I thought I had more time to finish up and sneak out."

Derrick sets me down gently, but no one moves. We're all exchanging glances like we're trying to silently assign someone to speak first.

She clears her throat and shifts Lillian on her hip. "I just… I know you've all been eating hospital food for days, and I wanted to help. I thought maybe I could do something good for once." Her voice cracks, just a little. "I know it's not my place."

Her eyes finally land on me—and the glassy sheen there nearly undoes me. It's not fake. It's not performative. It's heartbreak.

"I'm glad you're okay, Marley," she says, voice trembling. "Your dad told me what he said to you. The ugly things. I'm so, so sorry."

"I just came to drop this little one off, make some breakfast, and get out of your way."

She sets Lillian down gently, and the moment her little feet hit the floor, she toddles straight to Jones like nothing's wrong—like the world hasn't tilted at all. Jones crouches to catch her, lifting her easily into his arms.

Jessica clears her throat again. She's nervous, twisting the corner of her apron between her fingers.

"Sev." Her voice wavers. "Sorry—Sevynn."

Sev straightens slightly, eyes cautious but not cold.

"I... I can't condone the things Jax said to Marley," Jessica continues, voice steadier now. "I won't stand for it. I've asked him to leave the house."

A hush falls again, heavier this time.

"I know that might not mean much, and I know it's not really your concern. But I needed you to hear it from me. I never want to see your kids hurt…again. Especially not because I stayed quiet."

She swallows, glancing at me, then back to Mom.

"I'll still bring Lillian anytime you want to see her. I won't keep her from her family. And I won't be part of anything—or anyone—that teaches her love comes with cruelty."

Damn. My respect for her ticks up a few notches. Didn't see that coming.

I step forward and pull her into a hug. Our first. Probably long overdue. The weight of old tension lifts just a little as her arms come around me. Better to let the animosity go. It's not healthy for any of us—not for Lillian, and not for me.

"That was a pretty fucking brave move, Jess. Respectable."

She nods, blinking fast as she wipes her cheeks. Grabs her purse, presses another kiss to Lillian's cheek while Jones holds her steady on one hip.

"Well done, Jessica," Jones says with a knowing wink. It's the first time he's *ever* used her actual name. Normally, it's some butchering of 'Jennifer' or 'Josephine' or 'Jazz Hands'—whatever would get under her skin. The fact that he didn't now? Yeah, she notices. Her breath catches like it's caught her off guard, too.

"You can stay and have breakfast with us," Mom says gently, stepping in before she can reach the door. "Stay."

Jessica offers a tired, grateful smile. "Let's give this all some time. I know my place here, Sevynn. I'm not foolish." She pauses, glancing around the room. "But know this—my heart and soul are heavy with regret. I mean that."

Her gaze drops to the counter.

"Enjoy the food. I used some of your recipes."

Then she's gone. Quietly. Leaving behind a room full of soft surprise and warm maple-syrup air.

Jessica surprised the ever-loving fuck out of me today. I could tell Sev was moved—maybe not ready to hand her a gold star, but moved. Nothing will ever undo the fact that Jessica played a part in wrecking Sev's life. But it's not all on her, either. Jaxon's been collecting women like cheap cufflinks for years. Jessica was just the latest in a long string of heartbreaks.

Still, she pulled out all the stops with brunch. Insisted on handling it solo. Told London's parents to sit down and enjoy themselves, said she had it covered—and damn, she *did*. Everything tasted incredible. Even Sev was practically licking her plate. No complaints, no snide remarks. Just chewing and nodding like her mouth was in church.

And then—

"So," London starts, setting his fork down, voice calm and calculated. "There's something Sev and I would like to discuss with all of you."

Oh shit.

Oh *fuckshit.*

I'm not ready.

Is it hot in here? Why does it suddenly feel like the fireplace kicked on, the oven's open, and I'm wearing a wool sweater sewn by Satan himself?

I rake both hands through my hair and glance around the room. Why are there *so many people* here? When did this house get so small? Why is everyone looking at me like I know what this is?

I *do* know what this is.

And I'm still not ready.

Sev takes London's hand, then reaches across the table and slips her fingers through mine.

"We've entered into a poly relationship," she says calmly, "with Jones."

A ripple of silence follows her words. Not awkward—just still. Intent. "It's probably been a long time coming," she adds. "And we're not asking for anyone's blessing or approval." Her gaze lands on London's parents—and lingers. They do, in fact, look like someone just clutched their pearls and passed the tray.

Mrs. Pierce clears her throat, eyebrows arching in concern more than judgment. "What does that mean, exactly?"

London doesn't flinch. Doesn't soften. He laces our hands together beneath the table, and speaks with a steady voice I know cost him everything to claim.

"It means I'm bisexual. I've known for as long as I can remember." A quiet inhale from his father. London doesn't stop.

"In college, I had a long-term relationship with Baxley. You knew him as my best friend. But he was more than that." His voice dips for just a moment, cracked by memory. "I loved him. And I lost him because I was too afraid to live honestly."

My throat tightens. Sev squeezes my hand.

"I'm in love with Jones. And I'm in love with Sev," London continues. "We've asked Jones to marry us. This is our future. This is the life we want. You don't have to understand it. But I won't hide who I am anymore."

His words settle like a thunderclap over the room.

Mr. and Mrs. Pierce glance at each other—just a flick of the eyes—but something shifts. Not rejection. Something closer to resignation, wrapped in love. A silent agreement to shove their outdated beliefs aside and choose their son. Wholly. As he is.

London's watching them like a man waiting to be struck—tense, braced, hopeful.

The silence thickens.

And then—**Lizzo**.

The speakers *blare* to life, mid-chorus, her voice echoing through the house like a divine punchline:

"It's about damn time! In a minute, I'ma need a sentimental man or woman to pump me up—"

Derrick, Simone, and Sloane come spinning into view like unhinged backup dancers, locked in some chaotic fusion of 'ring-around-the-rosie' and full-body twerk. Simone is holding her hands up and still somehow missing the beat. Derrick's shirt is half-buttoned and open like he's starring in a low-budget 90s R&B video.

Marcus and Joe are already on their feet, pumping fists, grinding the air with zero shame and *far* too much commitment. Joe mouths the lyrics like it's a concert. Marcus drops it low enough to threaten a permanent back injury.

Sev bursts out laughing. London's mouth twitches. Marley leans his back against Remi, arms crossed, watching the circus unfold with the resigned amusement of a man who's seen this movie before.

And me? I'm just staring, half in awe, half in disbelief, thinking:

This is my family now. What the actual fuck. And thank God.

London's mom is the first to move. She steps out from behind the kitchen island, her hands trembling just slightly, and pulls him into a hug that feels like the end of a long war.

The dam breaks.

London clutches her, burying his face in her shoulder as the sobs take him under. Years of restraint, silence, fear—flooding out all at once.

"I'm sorry you ever thought we wouldn't love and support you, mijo," she whispers, voice cracking. She pulls back just enough to cup his cheeks and wipe her tears with shaking fingers. "*Te amo, mi amor.* All of you. Every part."

Before London can answer, his father rounds the corner and yanks him into a hug so tight, so crushing, it turns both their faces red. He doesn't say a word—he doesn't have to. The way he holds his son says everything.

And I realize I'm gripping the edge of the counter, jaw

tight, heart fucking full. Because this? This is what redemption looks like.

This is what home feels like.

"It's about damn time," Marley says, clapping a hand to my shoulder, grin wide and eyes suspiciously glassy.

Before I can respond, Simone's voice cuts through the moment like a firework.

"Speaking of announcements…" she pants, red-faced from dancing but glowing all the same. She raises both fists in the air. "We're having a baby!"

The room detonates.

Cheers, tears, shrieks, bodies colliding in hugs and laughter. Lillian buries her face in my neck and slaps her tiny hands over her ears, unimpressed by the decibel level. Even London's parents are teary-eyed, holding each other in stunned joy.

Simone, never one to let a spotlight cool, grabs Derrick's hand with a wicked grin. "Derrick, go ahead and tell your mom the name you *insist* on her being called."

"You *snitch!*" he yells, clutching his chest like he's been mortally wounded. "I confided in you!"

"Go. On." Her grin widens.

Derrick sighs dramatically, then turns to Sev with the expression of a man bracing for impact.

"Well. You're not like other moms, you know?"

"Uh huh." Sev folds her arms, smirking.

"You like beer. You lift. You're tatted. Cool as fuck. I just…

I can't picture a kid calling you *Grandma*."

"Uh huh."

He winces. "So, I said... maybe the baby could call you... *G-Unit*."

Simone loses it. The room does, too.

Sev just stares at him.

"I'm gonna have that embroidered on a damn diaper bag," she mutters, shaking her head—then she walks over and throws her arms around him.

And just like that, the night becomes a memory we'll all carry until the end.

"Hey."London's voice slips into my ear, low and steady, cutting right through the laughter and chaos like it was meant just for me.

I turn toward him, and he's smiling—really smiling. Big and unguarded, the kind of smile that reaches his eyes and lodges itself straight in my chest.

"Hey, yourself," I murmur.

His hand finds my jaw, thumb brushing the edge of my beard, and then he kisses me. Soft. Sure. In front of everyone.

No more secrets. No hesitation. He's claiming me—out loud, in the open—and I swear my fucking heart forgets how to beat.

"All in?" he asks.

I nod, breath catching. "All in."

Then he's dropping to one knee.

The room shifts. The noise fades.

London pulls a ring from his pocket—a simple, flawless gold Dior band with a single diamond, understated but screaming *intent*.

"All in," he says again, gaze locked on mine.

I hold out my hand, and it's shaking like hell, but I don't care. "All in, London, baby."

Marley...

"Fucking hell."

The words scrape out of my throat like gravel. My head is pounding—like there's a marching band in steel-toe boots stomping around inside my skull.

"Remi," I groan, rolling onto my side. My tongue feels like cotton. My stomach's doing barrel rolls. "I'm hungover. This is why I haven't drunk in years."

From beside me, there's a low grunt of agreement. "Yeah," Remi rasps, voice just as rough. "But what an *epic* fucking wedding that was."

I blink against the morning light leaking through the curtains. I don't even remember getting to the room last night. My tux jacket's on the floor, shoes in opposite corners of the suite, and there's confetti in the bed. *Actual confetti.*

"I don't remember anything past the third round of shots," I mutter, throwing an arm over Remi's bare stomach. "Did we...?" I glance down, then up. "Yeah, we definitely did."

Remi shifts under the sheets with a wince. "You left the shower running."

My eyes flick to the bathroom door.

"I didn't take a shower," I say slowly.

We both freeze.

The sound of water stops.
We sit up at the same time—joints popping, breaths held. A sense of *oh no* crashing down on us like a slow-moving freight train.

We look at each other. Then at the space around us.

This isn't our hotel room.

There are clothes everywhere. Not just ours. Women's clothes. Lacy. Strappy. Shiny.
There's an empty bottle of champagne tipped over on the nightstand. Two more on the floor.
Condom wrappers. At least five. Glitter. A bra hanging from the ceiling fan.

I run a hand through my hair like that'll somehow comb the memory back into place. "Remi… what the fuck happened?"

"I don't know," he says, eyes darting around as he stands up, sheet barely hanging onto his hips. "Oh God. I think we hosted an orgy."

"No," I whisper, heart thudding. "No. No. *Nooooo.*" I groan, dragging a hand down my face. "*Not again.*"

The bathroom door creaks open.

And there she is.

Sloane.

London's baby fucking sister, Sloane.

Wrapped in nothing but a fluffy white towel and smug satisfaction. Her skin is dewy, flushed from the heat of the shower, hair wet and curling over her shoulders. She leans against the doorframe like it's her stage, one brow arched, eyes sparkling with secrets and sin.

"Hey, boys." Her grin could melt glaciers.

My jaw drops. Remi actually *whimpers*.

And then a flash. A blink of memory: my hand in her hair. Her mouth on Remi. Her hips rocking between us. Her moans—guttural and goddamn *committed*.

I slap my palm to my forehead like it'll knock the image loose. "Oh God. We Eiffel Towered London's sister!"

Sloane tilts her head. "That's not the weirdest thing we did last night."

Remi lets out a strangled sound. "*That wasn't* the weirdest thing we did last night?!"

"Nope."

He sits back down on the bed, throws an arm over his face, and groans like the weight of the world is suddenly on his chest. "I need to lie down. Forever."

"Good shower," she says, stretching like a fucking cat— languid and smug, like she didn't just lob a nuclear bomb into our already-fried brains.

"What the actual fuck, Sloane?" I go to run my hand through my hair, desperate for some kind of grounding. And then I freeze. There's an extra ring on my finger. This one's silver. Twisted. Familiar.

"What the actual *fuck*, Sloane," I say again, louder, holding my hand out like it's evidence in a goddamn trial.

She smirks, padding toward the bed with zero shame and a towel that's holding on by hope and humidity. "You both said yes," she singsongs. "I have video."

Remi jerks up like a corpse brought back to life. He looks down at his hand. Another ring. Matching.

"Oh my God," he whispers. "We're all married now?!"

She shrugs. "Vegas rules, baby."

I flop back onto the mattress like a man awaiting judgment. "I'm dead. I'm a fucking *dead man*. We need an annulment. Or a lawyer. Or both."

"Or breakfast," she says cheerfully, climbing under the covers between us. "But first…" She wedges herself in with practiced ease, tossing an arm around my waist, and dragging Remi's arm over hers. "Huggies with my hubbies."

Remi groans. I stare at the ceiling like it holds answers.

And just like that, the chaos resumes.

Still recovering from this chaos?

Buckle up. The final chapter unfolds with Derrick, Simone, Marley, and Remi in *The Guest Book*—the last book in the Reckless Hearts Series—coming Spring 2026!

Need more Remi and Marley? Their story unfolds Summer 2026 in 'LeVeaux'